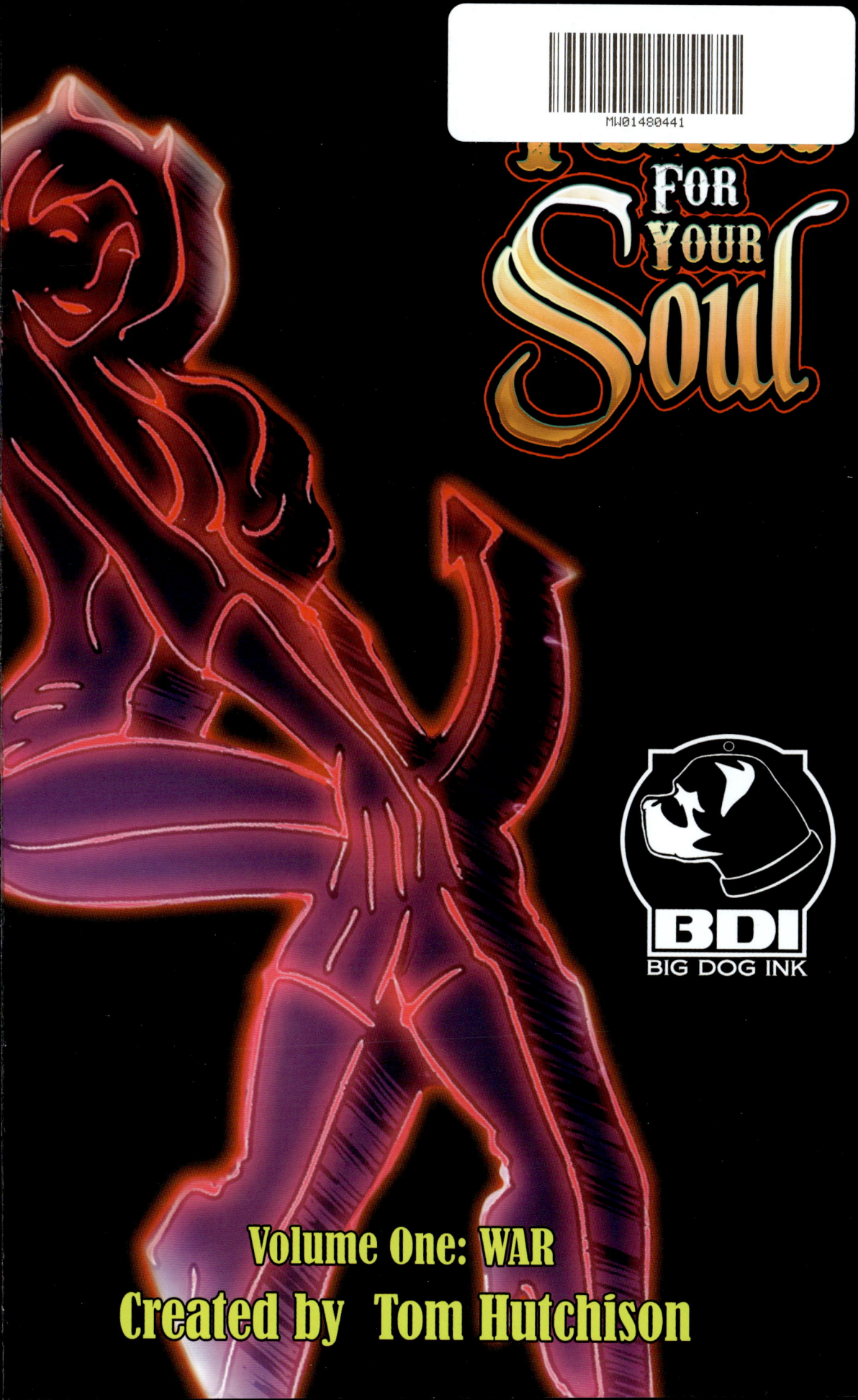

FOR YOUR Soul

BDI
BIG DOG INK

Volume One: WAR
Created by Tom Hutchison

Writer
Tom Hutchison

Penciler and Inker
J.B. Neto

Color Artist and Letters
Oren Kramek

Cover Artist
Joe Jusko

Original Series Alternate Covers

Eric Basaldua, Fico Ossio, Mike DeBalfo

Rob Duenas, Corey Knaebel, Greg Smallwood

Nei Ruffino, Monte Moor, Lessa Michelle

Armando Huerta

Epilogue Artists

Edson Novais & Alzir Alves, Mannix & Shi Peng Li

Mike Vosburg & Shi Peng Li, Alisson Borges & Kate Finnegan

Ian Snyder & Kate Finnegan

PENNY FOR YOUR SOUL VOLUME ONE: WAR. July 2011. Published by Big Dog Ink. Office of publication: 424 S. Dunton Ave Arlington Heights Il 60005. Copyright © 2011 Tom Hutchison. All rights reserved. PENNY FOR YOUR SOUL (including all prominent characters featured herin), it's logo and all character likenesses are trademarks of Tom Hutchison unless otherwise noted. No part of this publication may be reproduced or transmitted, in any form or by any means (except for short excerpts for review purposes) without the express written permission of Tom Hutchison. All names, characters, events and locales in this publication are entirely fictional. Any resemblance to actual persons (living or dead), events or places, without satiric intent, is coincidental.

PENNY FOR YOUR SOUL

Forward by Michel Dolce

What you're holding in your hands is so much more than a mere comic book. It's more than an epic struggle between Heaven and Hell weaved togther to perfection by Tom Hutchison. And it's greater than the stunning renditions from J.B. Neto and Oren Kramek. It may not seem that way to the untrained eye, but believe me it is. What you're holding is the culmination of a mountain of hard work, preparation and quite simply a love for the medium that is the Indie Comic scene. Let's rewind a bit shall we?

I first met Tom almost 5 years ago, peddling my Indie baby THE SIRE at Wizard World L.A. Tom had approached my Artists Alley table not only as a fan of the book, but more importantly as an aspiring creator himself. He wanted to know, as many others in the same position I've come across in my ten years in the biz, what steps need to be taken to publish one's own comic book. The first and most important step I told him was to just do it. Get it done. Get your words on paper, track down an artist and just do it. Simple, I know, but you'd be surprised how often I've come across exactly the same type of person with the exact same type of questions. And when I revisit different cons year after year, I'd run into those exact same people still stuck at square one, each packing a different set of reasons (excuses?) as to why they hadn't been able to get their project off the ground.

But not Tom. He my friends, was the exception in this case. Not the rule.

As we kept in touch over the years, I got to sit back and smile wide and watch a kindred spirit build the foundations for what is now PENNY FOR YOUR SOUL -- a labor of love that is reflected in each page, each panel. It's something that can easily be taken for granted by the causal reader only because many have no idea how hard it can be getting something off the ground, let alone creating something of any lasting significance in this industry. But, with the help of a talented group of artists, Tom & company pulled it off and pulled it off with syle.

So enjoy the first volume of PENNY FOR YOUR SOUL. Guaranteed to stimulate your eyes as well as your brain, this will be the first of many more trades to come. I should know, I got to watch it come together from the front row. And the next time I see Tom at a con, I'll get to approach his table, not only as a friend, but as a fan as well.

DAY
WELCOME
TO Fabulous
LAS VEGAS
NEVADA
MANDALAY
Las Vegas
Sin City
My kind of place.
A city built on the idea that anything goes and anyone can win.
The men who come here dream of money, sex and anonymity as they gamble, drink and spend their paychecks while trying to coerce any hot chick that will listen to be their personal party girl.
Even though this type of lifestyle comes with a price, that is what they consider winning.
My idea of winning is a little different.
Though I'll admit there's nothing wrong with a hot chick to party with.
Of course the only one who ever truly wins in this town...
...is me!

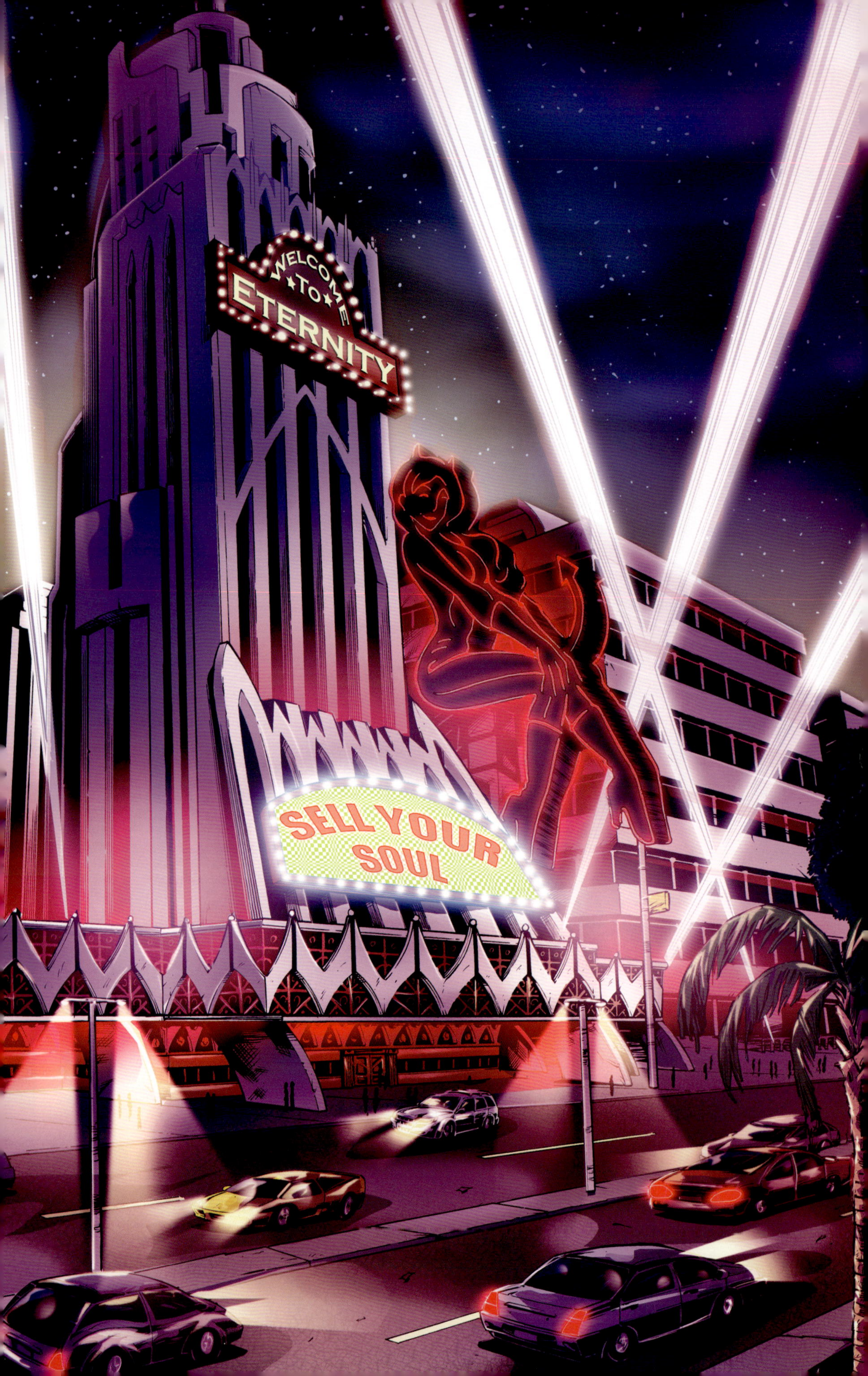
WELCOME TO ETERNITY
SELL YOUR SOUL

WELCOME TO THE ETERNITY HOTEL SIR. ARE YOU STAYING WITH US TONIGHT?
YES I HAVE RESERVATIONS.
WELL THAT'S WONDERFUL! CHECK IN IS TO YOUR RIGHT AS YOU ENTER THE HOTEL AND THE CASINO IS TO THE LEFT.
THANK YOU...UH...
BUNNY!
BUNNY? ARE YOU KIDDING?
NOPE. MOM DIED IN CHILDBIRTH AND DADDY WAS A PERV. SO HEEEERE'S BUNNY.
IS THAT A NORMAL NAME FOR LAS VEGAS?
OH I'M NOT FROM VEGAS. I'M FROM UTAH! BYE NOW
BYE... BUNNY.

WELCOME TO THE ETERNITY HOTEL SIR.
DON'T FORGET TO SELL YOUR SOUL BEFORE YOU HIT THE CASINO!
WHAT DID YOU JUST SAY?
~SELL YOUR ~SOUL!~
$10,000
IS WAITING FO
YOU JUST FOR
SIGNING UP W
CASINO REWA
ALL YOU HAV
TO DO IS SELL
YOUR SOUL!

THIS IS WHAT I'VE BEEN HEARING ABOUT?

CAN I HELP YOU SIR?

WHOA!

WHERE'D YOU COME FROM?

UTAH SOUND RIGHT?

LET'S SEE IF WE CAN GET YOU SOME CREDIT MR. ANDERSON. AND MAKE SURE YOUR STAY WITH US IS AS PLEASURABLE AS POSSIBLE.

HOW DID YOU KNOW MY NAME?

"IT'S MY BUSINESS TO KNOW MY GUESTS, AND I'D SAY YOU'RE HERE BECAUSE THE WIFE BACK HOME ISN'T QUITE THE HELLCAT SHE WAS IN COLLEGE."

"WELL... WAIT A MINUTE. HOW DO YOU KNOW THAT?"

"SO FEW MEN ARE WILLING TO ADMIT THEIR NEEDS AND DESIRES. BUT I CAN TELL YOU ARE DIFFERENT MR. ANDERSON."

"THAT STILL DOESN'T ANSWER MY QUESTION."

"I'M GOING TO INTRODUCE YOU TO SOMEONE VERY SPECIAL MR. ANDERSON."

"SHE IS GOING TO GET YOU SIGNED UP WITH OUR REWARDS CLUB AND GET YOU YOUR MONEY AND MAKE SURE YOU HAVE A GOOD TIME FOR AS LONG AS YOU'RE HERE."

"THAT SOUNDS WONDERFUL... UH..."

"I'M SO SORRY. I'M DANICA..."

"...FROM UTAH."

"NOW LET'S SELL THAT SILLY LITTLE SOUL OF YOURS SO YOU CAN HAVE SOME FUN, COMPLIMENTS OF THE ETERNITY HOTEL AND CASINO."

WELL HELLO THERE. CAN I HELP YOU SELL YOUR SOUL TODAY?
HI...
THANK YOU ELIZABETH, BUT WE ARE HERE TO SEE MAGGIE.
OKIE DOKIE.
HI DANICA. BRING ME SOMEONE SPECIAL DID YOU?
WE GET THOUSANDS OF PEOPLE THROUGH HERE EVERY DAY.
ALL OF THEM WILLING TO SELL THEIR SOUL FOR TEN THOUSAND DOLLARS.
MOST TAKE THE MONEY AND PISS IT AWAY ON OVER PRICED FOOD AND RIDICULOUS SOUVENIRS.
THE REALLY DUMB ONES PLOP THAT MONEY ON A TABLE IN THE CASINO. NONE OF THESE PEOPLE KNOW WHAT THEY WANT. BUT YOU...
YOU ARE HERE FOR A VERY SPECIAL TYPE OF EXPERIENCE
AM I RIGHT?

"WE KNOW EXACTLY WHAT YOU CAME TO LAS VEGAS FOR MR. ANDERSON AND WE ARE READY, WILLING AND ABLE TO ACCOMMODATE YOU."

"ALL YOU HAVE TO DO IS SIGN UP FOR OUR ETERNITY REWARDS CLUB AND YOU WILL RECEIVE TEN THOUSAND DOLLARS TO DO WITH WHAT YOU WISH."

"YOU CAN GAMBLE, EAT, DRINK..."

"...OR IS THIS MORE WHAT YOU HAD IN MIND?"

"HI."

"TWO DAYS WITH A GIRL LIKE THIS IN ONE OF OUR SINNERS SUITES WOULD COST ROUGHLY TEN THOUSAND DOLLARS."

"ANY IDEA WHERE YOU CAN GET THAT KIND OF MONEY IN A HURRY?"

"THANK YOU MR. ANDERSON. I'LL TAKE THIS..."

"...AND YOU TAKE THIS."

"NOW IN ORDER TO GET TO YOUR ROOM, YOU'RE GOING TO HAVE TO GO STRAIGHT THROUGH THE CASINO THEN VEER TO YOUR LEFT."

"TAKE A SHARP RIGHT AT THE FIRST GIANT FERN I IMPORTED FROM THE AMAZON JUNGLE AND YOU'LL SEE A BANK OF POKER SLOT MACHINES."

"NOT BLACKJACK SLOT MACHINES, POKER SLOT MACHINES. TAKE ANOTHER RIGHT INTO THE SHOPPING PLAZA AND THEN WIND AROUND TO YOUR LEFT."

"IF YOU GET TO THE GARDEN OF HEDON YOU'VE GONE TO FAR SO BACK UP AND TAKE ANOTHER RIGHT. THEN KEEP WALKING AND YOU'LL SEE A BANK OF ELEVATORS."

"GOLD ELEVATORS, THOSE ARE YOURS. TAKE THEM UP TO THE TENTH FLOOR, TAKE A RIGHT AND AT THE END OF THE HALLWAY YOU'LL FIND YOUR ROOM."

THANK YOU, DANICA.

OH MR. ANDERSON...

YOU FORGOT YOUR PET.

THAT'S OUR ONE HUNDREDTH SIGN UP OF THE DAY, DAN.

DON'T CALL ME DAN.

DON'T CALL ME MAGGIE.

WELL I'M NOT CALLING YOU MARY. SHOULD I CALL YOU GRAIL?

FORGET IT. MAGGIE'S FINE.

SORRY. WHEN'S THE LAST TIME YOU TALKED TO HIM?

COUPLE YEARS AGO. NOT SINCE YOU MADE ME HOTEL MANAGER.

I STILL CAN'T BELIEVE HE LEFT HEAVEN TO DO THAT RADIO SHOW EVERY SUNDAY.

SAME OLD JESUS. CAN'T LIVE WITHOUT THE ATTENTION OF THE MASSES.

DID YOU TELL HIM WHAT WE'RE DOING HERE?

OF COURSE NOT.

LOOK, MAGS. YOU NEED TO GET PAST HIM. IF HE REALLY CARED ABOUT YOU, I WOULDN'T HAVE HAD TO PULL YOU OUT OF PURGATORY.
I KNOW THERE'S A LOT OF HISTORY BETWEEN YOU TWO, AND ALL THAT DA VINCI STUFF CAN'T HELP BUT BRING UP MEMORIES THAT ARE CENTURIES OLD.
BUT JESUS, MAGGIE...YOU NEED TO GET LAID!
IS THAT AN OFFER?
WHY NOT MAKE IT A WAGER?
IF I WIN YOU HAVE TO RIDE THE BULL TONIGHT.
AND IF I WIN?
I SIGN OVER THE ETERNITY TO YOU.
AND WHAT PRAY TELL IS THE WAGER?
HOW ABOUT THIS?
THE NEXT PERSON THAT WALKS THOUGH THE V.I.P. DOOR WILL BE PUTTING DOLLAR BILLS IN MY PANTIES BY MIDNIGHT TONIGHT.

DONE.

YOU DO KNOW I HAVE THE V.I.P. GUEST LIST RIGHT?

I HOPE YOU HAVE THE PROPER ATTIRE FOR THE BULL TONIGHT.

-GIGGLE-

NO WAY. GOOD ONE MAGS.

SO LET'S CLARIFY.

YOU HAVE PRECISELY THREE AND A HALF HOURS TO GET A 40 YEAR OLD NUN WITH AN ADMITTEDLY IMPRESSIVE SET OF TITS TO STUFF YOUR UNDOUBTEDLY WET PANTIES WITH WADS OF CASH OR THIS GRAND MONUMENT TO SEX, DRUGS AND ROCK AND ROLL IS ALL MINE.

DID I GET THAT RIGHT?

YOU KISSED THE HOLY SAVIOR WITH THAT MOUTH?

I'LL HAVE YOU KNOW MY MOUTH GOT NO COMPLAINTS, THANK YOU.

I'LL HAVE TO PUT THAT TO THE TEST SOME DAY.

GOOD EVENING MA'AM AND WELCOME TO THE ETERNITY HOTEL.

MY GOODNESS, YOU ARE QUITE WELL DRESSED FOR A CONCUBINE OF ETERNAL EVIL.

I AM LOOKING FOR THE OWNER OF THIS HOUSE OF SIN.

I already know I've lost the bet. It won't take long for her to start in with her "Life Is For Living" speech.
Not even a nun will be able to resist it. Maybe her being a nun will actually make it resonate more.
She's gotten good at this, that's for sure. She is her father's daughter.
She's already got the boys behind her so she can wag her tight ass for them.
She's right too, I suppose. Life is worth living. Eternal Peace or Eternal Hell is no choice anyone on this planet should have to make considering the living conditions.
A real silver tongued devil.
ARE YOU LITTLE MISS MAGGIE? I WAS TOLD TO SEE YOU TO GET MY MONEY.
WANT TO SELL YOUR SOUL DO YOU?
HELL YEAH! IT'S LIKE FREE MONEY! I DON'T KNOW HOW YOU GUYS ARE ABLE TO DO THIS BUT I'M READY TO SIGN UP!

YOU DO KNOW YOU'RE ACTUALLY SELLING YOUR SOUL RIGHT?
HA HA! YEAH. WHATEVER.
THAT MEANS WHEN YOU DIE YOU DON'T GO TO HEAVEN.
BUT YOU DO GET TO AVOID HELL I SUPPOSE.
UH HUH.
IT MEANS WHEN YOU DIE YOU COME HERE. YOU WORK FOR US. FOR ETERNITY. THAT WORK FOR YOU?
IF I GET TO WORK WITH YOU IT DOES.
I'LL SEE WHAT I CAN DO.
ALRIGHT MR. MORGAN, HERE IS YOUR TEN THOUSAND DOLLARS. YOU MAY USE IT ANYWHERE IN THE HOTEL OR CASINO.
NOW I'VE GOT A LINE BUILDING SO WHY DON'T YOU GO HAVE A LITTLE FUN.
TEN THOUSAND ON BLACK! HA HA HA HA!
Danica is right. Everyone has a price.
But what's really interesting is that she seems to have set that price remarkably low, especially for this town. But I guess the guys in marketing were right too...

BULL RIDING CONTEST TONIGHT IN THE GARDEN OF HEDON ROOM

...Sex sells!

COME AND GET ME BOYS...

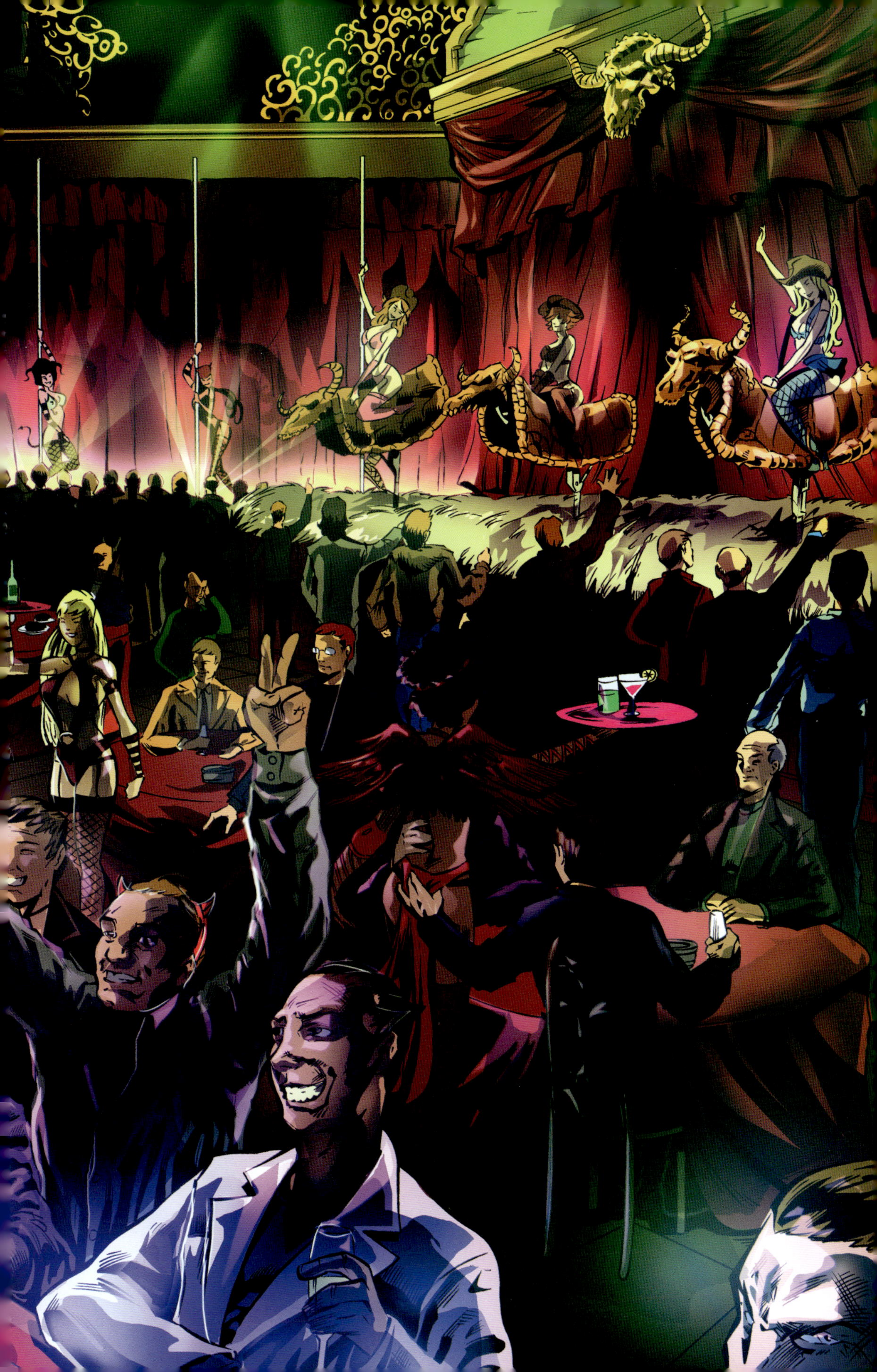

"...AND GIRLS!"

"Heathen bitch."

"Is there no one on this God forsaken planet that can resist her wiggling?"

"Ugh. Guess I should watch that glass house I'm living in."

Well...When in Rome...

LET'S RIDE!

"EVERYTHING IS WORKING OUT SO WELL. I CAN'T BELIEVE IT'S ONLY TAKEN FIVE YEARS TO BUILD THIS LITTLE EMPIRE."

"IT SOMETIMES DOESN'T EVEN SEEM REAL."

"THAT'S MY GIRL."

"BUT I KNOW THAT DAY WILL COME WHEN SOMEONE ABOVE OR BELOW WILL TAKE NOTICE. THAT'S WHEN IT WILL REALLY GET INTERESTING."

WHAM

"JESUS CHRIST!"

"WHAT THE HELL?"

"CLOSE. THINK MORE...SOUTHERN. BUT WITHOUT THE ACCENT."

"DADDY?"

Looks like Danica was right.

A little bit of Hell just broke loose on a Tuesday night.

Next Issue:
Father vs Daughter
Angels vs Demons
......and......
Jesus Christ Superstar!

Epilogue...

There's an age old saying going back to the time of the caveman...

IF YOU LIKE...

...I'LL LEAD THE WAY, SIR.

I'LL FOLLOW YOU ANYWHERE, PET.

"Men are pigs".
Ok so maybe that saying doesn't quite come from the Neanderthal women who got dragged off to caves by their hair, but it's true nonetheless.

It's really no secret that men not only love to own pretty little toys...

...but also get immense satisfaction at being able to show off their "prowess".

FORGIVE ME SIR.

GOOD GIRL. LEAD ON.

This ultimately is a perfect symbiotic relationship as each party is getting what they desire.

That being said however, I have always believed that there is a flip side to that swine coin.

It seems to me that the same women who call men pigs are themselves... piglets.

While the boys are hungry for control, the girls are hungry for the attention.

And why shouldn't they be allowed to have their fun?

This world is filled with bullshit. From asinine wars to economic apocalypse to simple minded people who think their idea of what's right is the only way to live and they have no problem ramming it down your throat on a daily basis.

And then there's the eternal question of whether you go up or down once your time here is done and it's based on the way you lived your life.

Wake up folks. You're being fooled.

Live your life following ten rules or down you go. That sounds a little strict if you ask me.

This planet has too much pain and to many assholes in charge of it to truly allow anyone a real opportunity to follow those rules and I say live your life how you want.

After all, going down isn't so bad...is it?

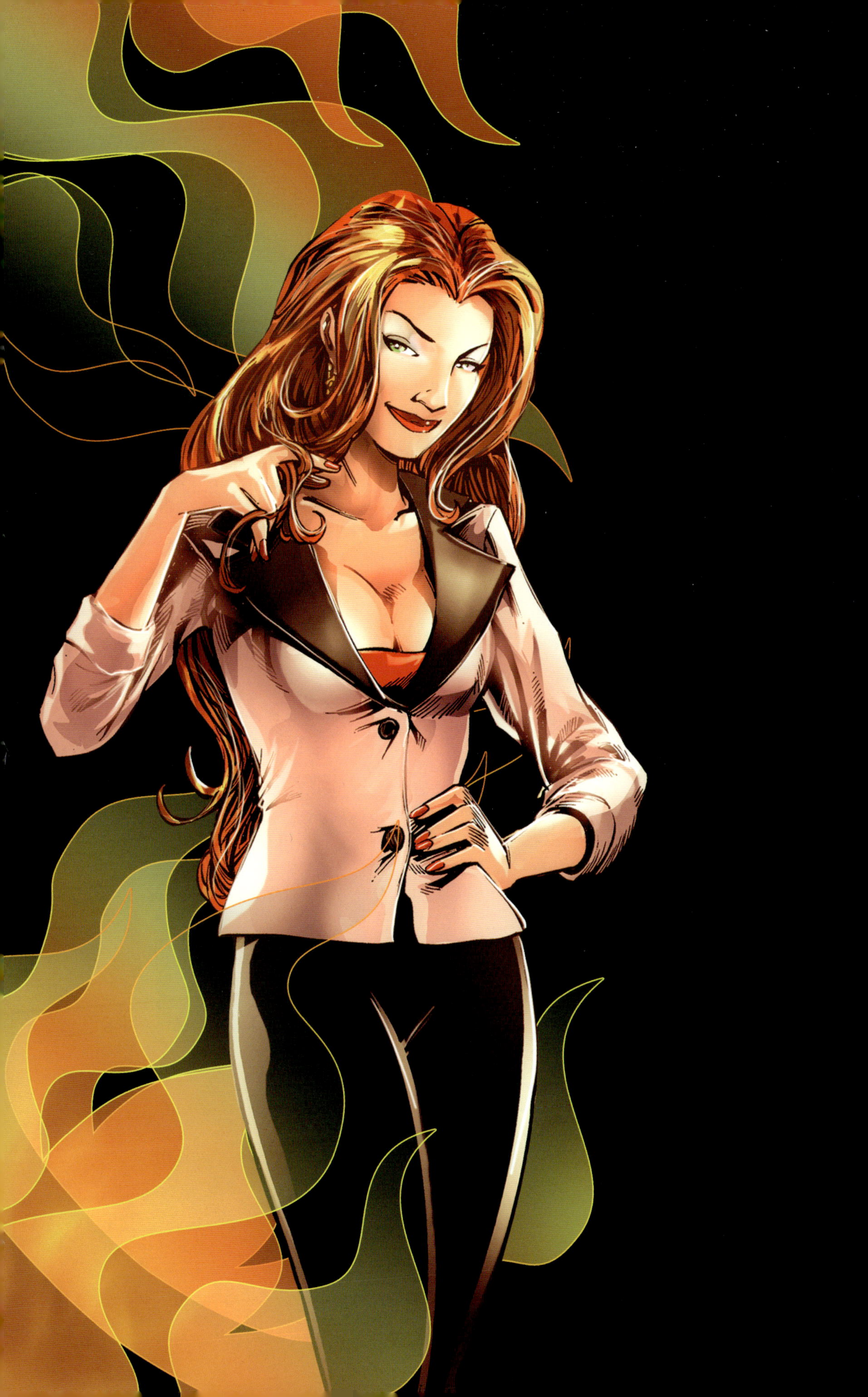

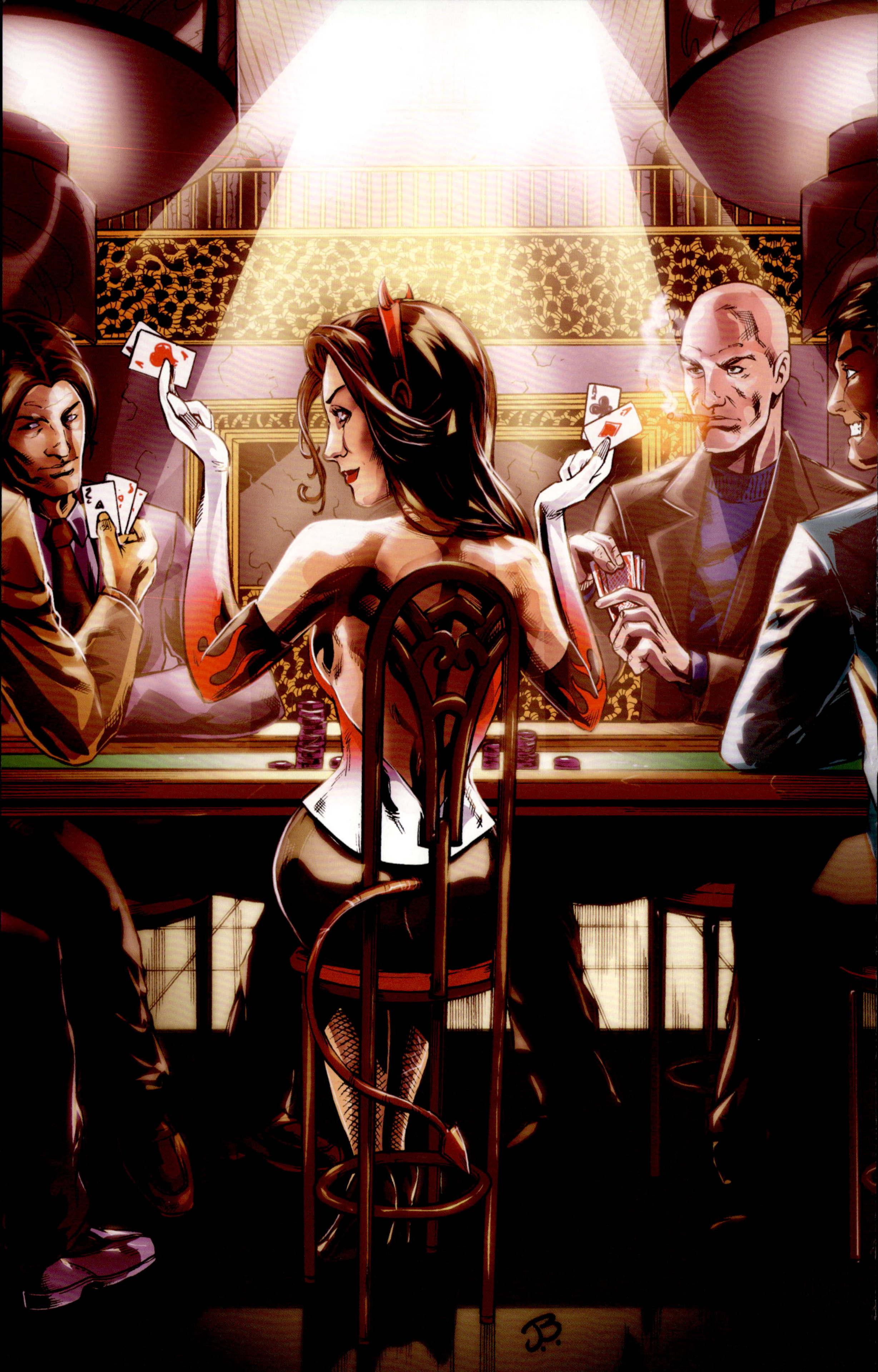

At first glance I guess you could say everything looks pretty normal around here. A Las Vegas hotel lit up to attract the insects that crawl out of the night.

But tonight a different kind of animal has shown up at our not-so-pearly-gates. Don't get me wrong, we don't mind raising a little Hell now and again. In fact we're somewhat famous for it here.

But this is the kind of Hell that no one wants crawling out of the darkness...

WELCOME TO ETERNITY

SELL YOUR SOUL

...this is the real thing.

YOU CAN'T JUST BLAST YOUR WAY INTO MY CLUB! THIS IS A PLACE OF BUSINESS!

THIS IS A PLACE OF DECADENCE DARLING. YOU HAD TO KNOW IT WOULD ATTRACT ME EVENTUALLY.

LOOK, IF YOU WANT TO SHOW UP, HAVE SOME DRINKS AND BANG SOME HUMAN CHICKS, THAT'S FINE AND DANDY. JUST GIVE ME SOME WARNING SO YOU DON'T SCARE MY GUESTS OUT OF THEIR MINDS AND OUT OF MY HOTEL!

YOU LOOK RIDICULOUS BY THE WAY. YOU'RE LIKE A PIMP FROM... WELL...FROM SOMEWHERE LAME.

COMING FROM THE POLE DANCER, I'LL TAKE THAT AS A COMPLIMENT.

SUCH A WILLFUL CHILD YOU ARE.

HEY!

WHAAA... MMMMM!

MMMMMM!!!
mmmmm...
EXCUSE ME! WE HAVE ROOMS FOR THIS KIND OF CONDUCT!
I APOLOGIZE. I SIMPLY CANNOT RESIST YOUR OUTFIT... DAUGHTER.
PIG...
THIS IS NOT FOR PUBLIC VIEW.
WE CAN CONTINUE THIS IN MY OFFICE.
SORRY ABOUT THE CAMERA. THESE ARE ON THE HOUSE.

"SO SPILL IT HUGGY BEAR. WHAT ARE YOU DOING HERE?"

"VERY DIRECT AREN'T YOU? RIGHT TO THE POINT, YES?"

"I WAS TOLD PLEASURE WAS THE FIRST RULE OF BUSINESS AT THE ETERNITY, BUT THAT WILL HAVE TO WAIT IT SEEMS. WE DO IT YOUR WAY... FOR NOW."

"YOU ARE PLAYING WITH COSMIC BALANCES THAT HAVE BEEN IN PLACE FOR MILLENNIA, MY SWEET."

"YOU HAVE NO HOLD ON ANYONE IN MY EMPLOY, FATHER. THEIR SOULS MAY BE EARMARKED FOR HEAVEN OR HELL, BUT IF THEY FREELY OFFER IT TO SOMEONE ELSE ALONG THE WAY..."

"YOUR PLUCKING OF SOULS FROM THIS EARTHLY PLANE HAS BEEN MINOR AND EVEN PERMITTED, BUT WE ARE NOW BEGINNING TO SEE MORE NOTICEABLE ABSENTEE'S DURING OUR DAILY ORIENTATIONS."

"YOU ARE COLLECTING SOULS THAT HAVE ALREADY BEEN SPOKEN FOR. I'M HERE TO COLLECT."

"YOU LOSE."

"DO NOT FORGET YOUR PLACE!"

"AS MY DAUGHTER YOU ARE ALSO MY PROPERTY. *WHAT* YOU OWN I OWN."

YOU...COUGH... GAVE UP YOUR RIGHTS TO ME... ACK...A LONG TIME AGO...
I'VE READ... YOUR RULE BOOK...
WHAM!
I KNOW YOUR GAME. YOURS AND HIS. FUCK YOUR COSMIC BALANCES. THERE'S A NEW PLAYER IN TOWN YOU GOAT HUMPING PIECE OF TRASH.
HA HA HA. THAT'S NO WAY TO TALK ABOUT YOUR MOTHER...
IN FACT I THINK I'LL KILL YOU JUST FOR THAT INSULT.
CLACK CLACK
CLACK
WHAT IS THIS?
CLACK
CLACK CLACK
WHAT THE HELL?
ANGELS?
IT'S AMAZING WHAT YOU CAN FIND IN PURGATORY.
THE EYE IN THE SKY SHOWED US YOU WERE HAVING A LITTLE TROUBLE. IS EVERYTHING ALL RIGHT IN HERE?

"PICK UP THIS SORRY EXCUSE FOR A FIRST BORN SON AND ESCORT HIM OUT OF MY HOTEL."

"YOU THINK KICKING ME OUT OF HERE WILL MAKE A DIFFERENCE, DANICA? I'M JUST THE BEGINNING OF YOUR PROBLEMS AND IF I KNOW WHAT YOU'RE DOING HERE, IT WON'T TAKE LONG FOR HIM TO KNOW AS WELL."

"GET HIM OUT OF HERE..."

"YES MA'AM..."

KRASSSHH!

"THAT WAS RUDE."

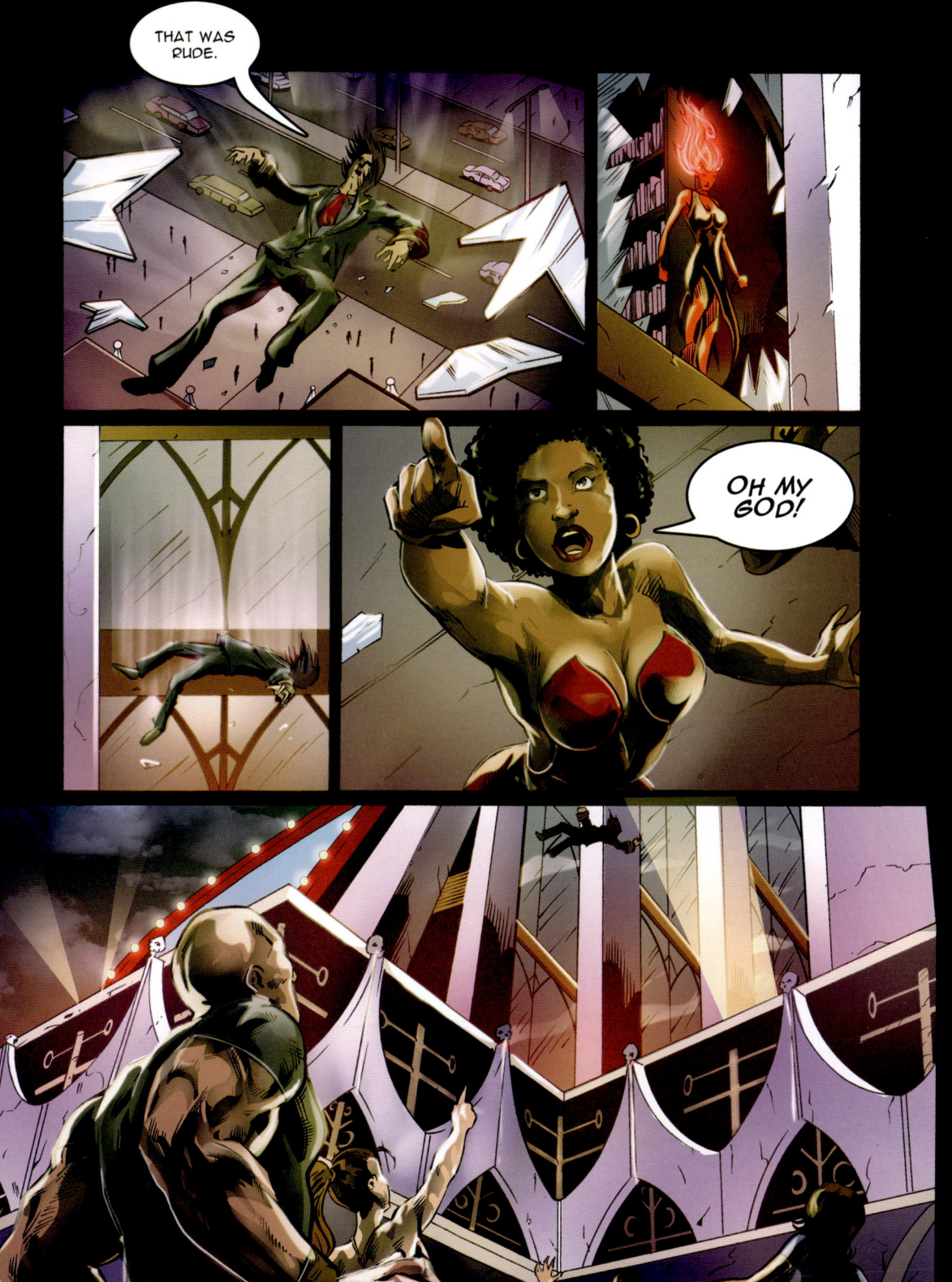

"OH MY GOD!"

EXPOSITUS PORTA INFERUS!

LOOK OUT!

WATCH IT!

WHAT'S HAPPENING?

WOW!

INCREDIBLE!

WHAT A SHOW!

...GREATEST STUNT I'VE SEEN!

HOW'D THEY DO THAT?

GOD DAMNED SHOW OFF.

ANYTHING FURTHER MA'AM?

YES. TAKE THAT USELESS DEMON TO THE BASEMENT AND GET WHATEVER INFORMATION YOU CAN OUT OF HIM. THEN RECYCLE HIM.

FRONT DESK...

-BLEEP-

I NEED HOTEL MAINTENANCE IN MY OFFICE ASAP.

RIGHT AWAY MA'AM.

"YOU OK DANICA?"

"I GUESS WE'LL KNOW THE ANSWER TO THAT SOON ENOUGH, WON'T WE?"

"I THOUGHT THIS WAS WHAT YOU WANTED? A SHOWDOWN BETWEEN YOU AND HELL, RIGHT? IT'S BEEN THE END RESULT OF YOUR GAME PLAN THE WHOLE TIME."

"I KNEW THIS DAY WAS COMING MARY."

"OF COURSE IT WAS. BUT NOW I QUESTION WHETHER WE'RE READY OR NOT."

"YOW! YOU WANNA TURN OFF THE HEAT FOR A WHILE?"

"SORRY MAGS."

"IT'S OK. YOU'RE SO TENSE. I'VE NEVER SEEN YOU THIS WOUND UP."

"WE HAVE TO GET EVERYONE TOGETHER FOR A STAFF MEETING. EVERYONE NEEDS TO BE ON THE SAME PAGE. THAT PIG OF A FATHER OF MINE COULD COME BACK ANY TIME AND BRING FAR WORSE THAN HIS PATHETIC LITTLE BODYGUARD."

"RELAX FOR A WHILE. CLEAR YOUR HEAD. LET ME HELP YOU."

SSS SSS

"I CAN'T RIGHT NOW. I NEED TO THINK..."

"SHUT UP FOR ONCE AND PRACTICE WHAT YOU PREACH."

-TAC-
-TAC-
-TAC-

"MAINTENANCE, MA'AM."

"DON'T MIND US BOYS. WE'LL BE DONE IN A MINUTE."

"YES MA'AM, NOT A PROBLEM. WE HAVE WORK TO DO ANYWAY."

Purgatory is full of them. Seems despite their service and ultimate sacrifice they ended up as a cosmic joke, left to rot for eternity with neither Heaven nor Hell wanting to claim them.

And what do I do with this cast out angel? I should be doing nothing more than giving her my total attention but for the first time in a long time my mind is...

Ah the devotion of a eunuch. They keep their eyes on the prize, and not my ass.

...somewhere else.

WELCOME TO HELL!
ONCE YOU ARE PROPERLY CHECKED IN YOU WILL BE ASSIGNED TO YOUR VARIOUS ETERNAL DAMNATIONS UNTIL THE DAY OF THE APOCALYPSE.
ON THAT GLORIOUS DAY YOU WILL BE CALLED INTO SERVICE AND GIVEN POSITIONS IN HELL'S ARMY AND WILL FIGHT THE WICKED ANGELS OF HEAVEN FOR THE ULTIMATE PRIZE...HELL ON EARTH.
DO YOU EVER GET TIRED OF GIVING THAT SPEECH?
GOOD BOY.
WELCOME HOME, LORD DAMIEN. HOW WAS YOUR TRIP?
NOT AS SATISFYING AS I HAD HOPED.
AHHH... THIS WILL DO.
I'LL NEED AN AUDIENCE WITH MY FATHER. WE HAVE THINGS TO DISCUSS.
OF COURSE, LORD DAMIEN. I WILL SEND A MESSENGER AHEAD FOR YOU AT ONCE.
SOON DEAREST DAUGHTER, YOU WILL BE SHOWN YOUR TRUE PLACE...

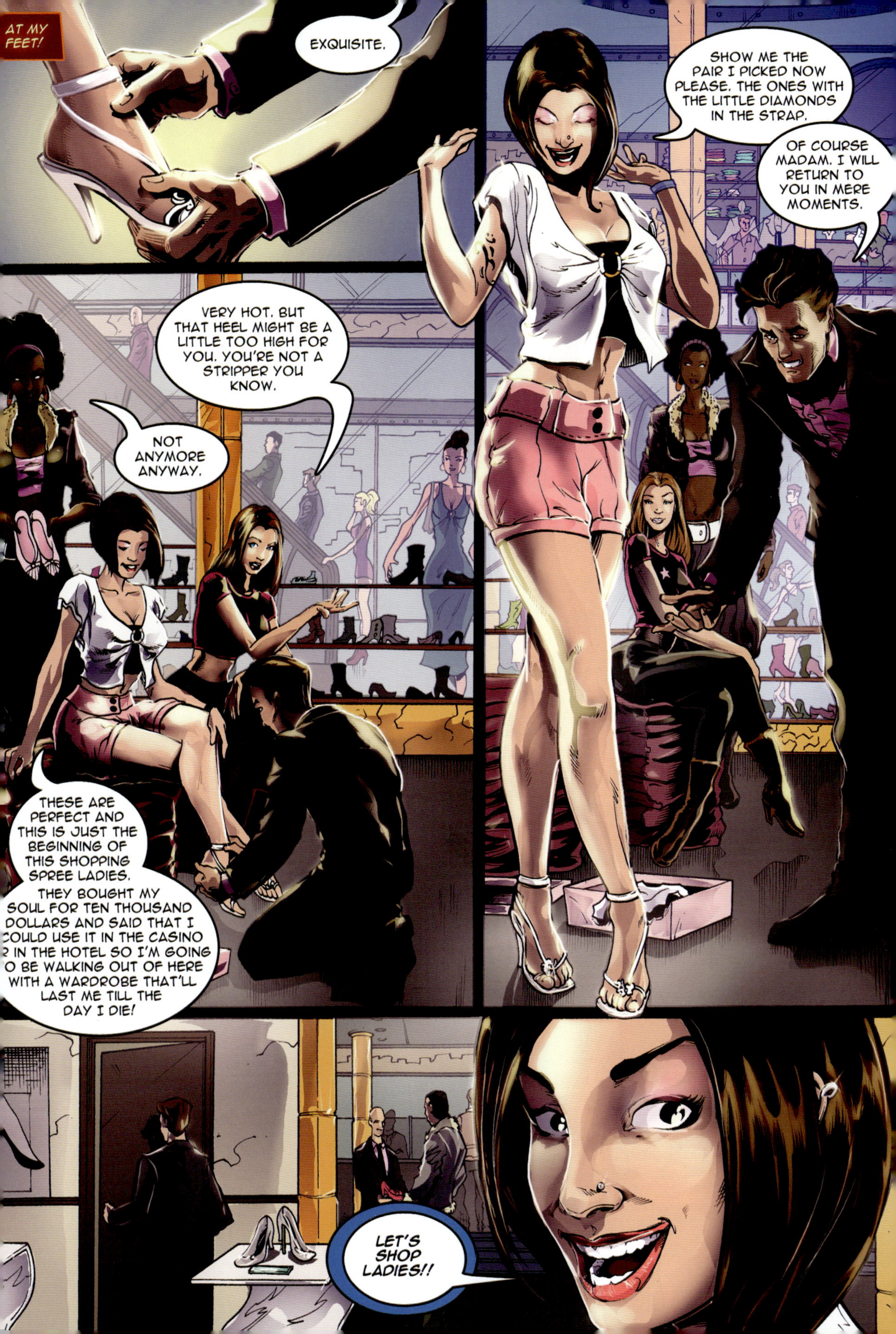
AT MY FEET!
EXQUISITE.
SHOW ME THE PAIR I PICKED NOW PLEASE. THE ONES WITH THE LITTLE DIAMONDS IN THE STRAP.
OF COURSE MADAM. I WILL RETURN TO YOU IN MERE MOMENTS.
VERY HOT. BUT THAT HEEL MIGHT BE A LITTLE TOO HIGH FOR YOU. YOU'RE NOT A STRIPPER YOU KNOW.
NOT ANYMORE ANYWAY.
THESE ARE PERFECT AND THIS IS JUST THE BEGINNING OF THIS SHOPPING SPREE LADIES.
THEY BOUGHT MY SOUL FOR TEN THOUSAND DOLLARS AND SAID THAT I COULD USE IT IN THE CASINO OR IN THE HOTEL SO I'M GOING TO BE WALKING OUT OF HERE WITH A WARDROBE THAT'LL LAST ME TILL THE DAY I DIE!
LET'S SHOP LADIES!!

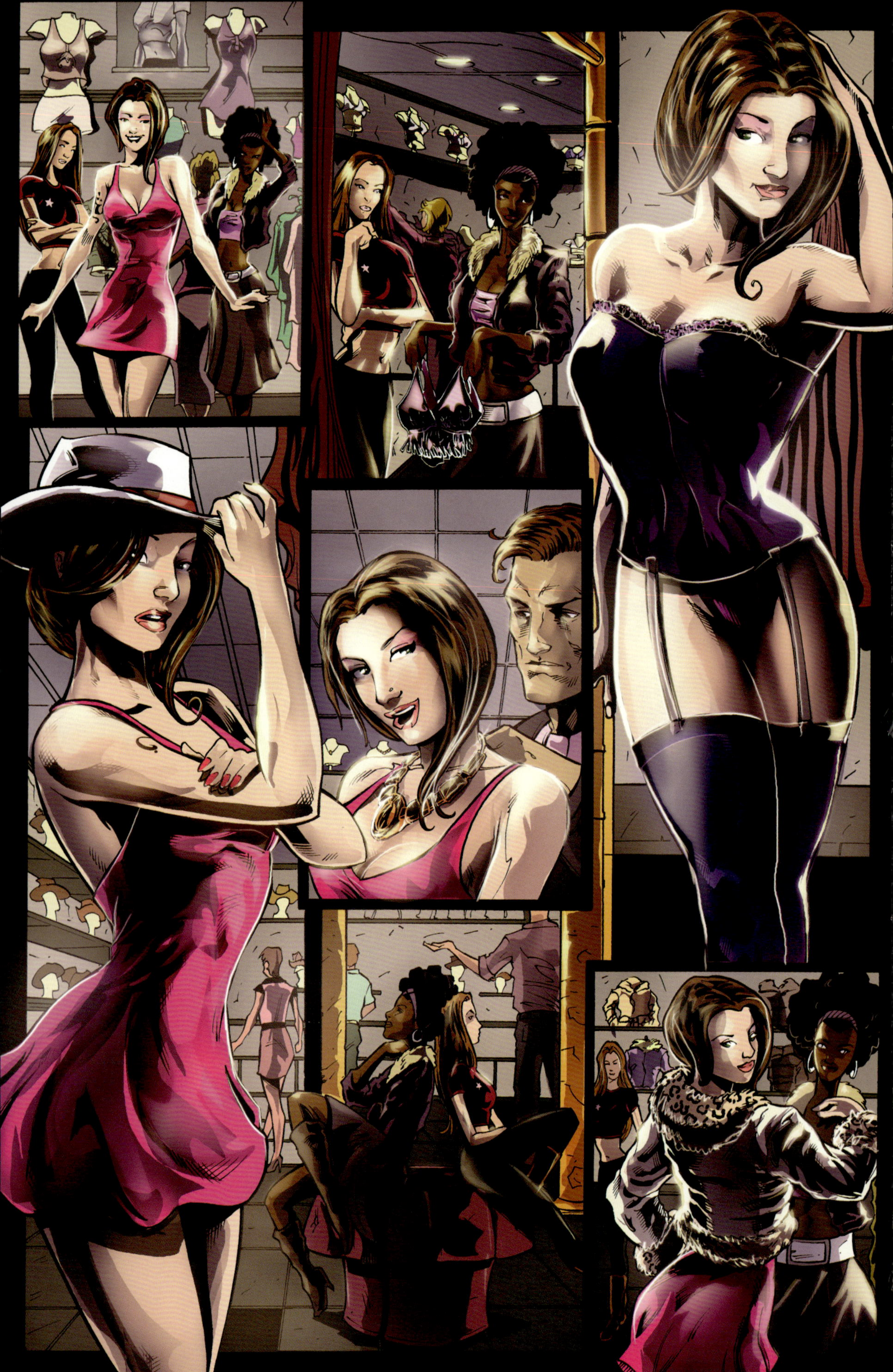

FABULOUS LADIES!

YEAH MAYBE FOR YOU.

YOU HAD YOUR CHANCE TO SELL YOUR SOUL TOO, MONICA.

WELL MAYBE MY SOUL ISN'T FOR SALE.

PLEASE. IT'S JUST A MARKETING SCHEME TO GET PEOPLE INTO THE HOTEL.

THE MEN WHO COME THROUGH HERE DUMP THEIR MONEY ON A CASINO TABLE OR DOWN A STRIPPER'S THONG, BUT IT TAKES A WOMAN'S INTELLECT TO REALIZE WHAT CAN BE TRULY DONE WITH THAT KIND OF CASH.

THEY GET A FEW HOURS OF FUN AND I GET A LIFETIME OF HIGH FASHION!

LET'S ROLL BITCHES!

LOOK OUT!

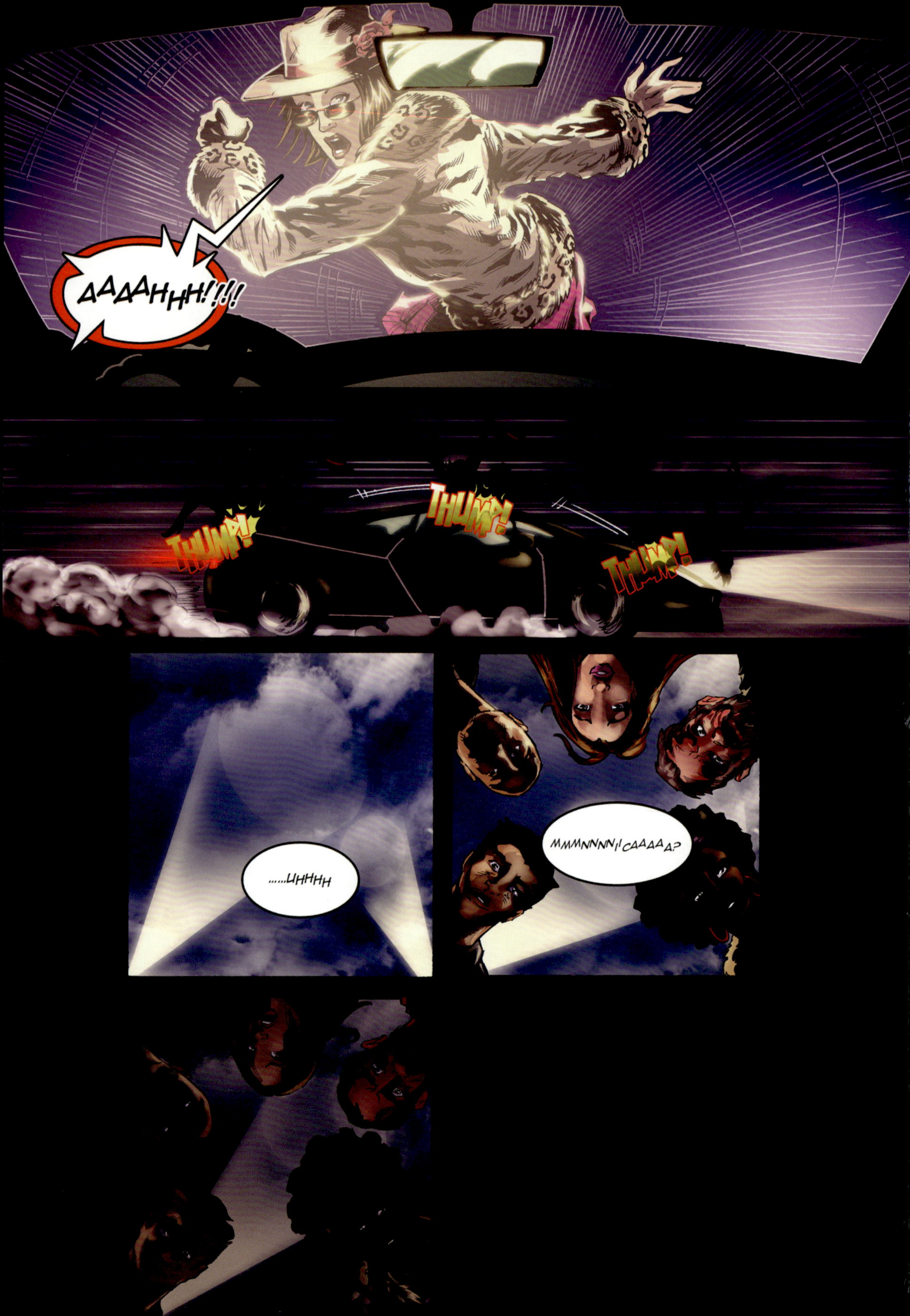
AAAAHHH!!!!
THUMP!
THUMP!
THUMP!
......UHHHH
MMMNNNNI'CAAAAA?

"I DIDN'T SIGN MYSELF OVER TO YOU GUYS TO BE TURNED INTO EYE CANDY FOR YOUR STUPID HOTEL!"

"THIS ISN'T FAIR!"

"...UHHHHH"

"LOOK SAM, I KNOW THIS IS CONFUSING RIGHT NOW BUT THE CONTRACT YOU SIGNED LETS US PUT YOUR SOUL IN ANY BODY TYPE WE SEE FIT."

"THIS IS BULLSHIT. I WANT TO SEE DANICA RIGHT NOW!"

"YOU'RE AWAKE? THAT WAS FAST. IT USUALLY TAKES A FEW HOURS TO COME OUT OF A DEATH SLEEP. I'LL HAVE TO NOTE THIS ON YOUR CHART."

"YES... SECURITY. I NEED YOU TO COLLECT A RECYCLED FEMALE WHO IS HEADING TOWARDS DANICA."

"UNDERSTOOD. WHAT'S SHE LOOK LIKE?"

"TRUST ME. YOU CAN'T POSSIBLY MISS HER."

"...MMMMNNNICAA?"

"HUH?"

"...DEAD?"

"YES MS. MCGEE. YOU WERE HIT BY A CAR ABOUT 30 MINUTES AGO AND AS PER YOUR CONTRACT YOUR SOUL WAS DEPOSITED IN OUR GUF. I LIKE TO USE A FACSIMILE OF A PERSON'S ORIGINAL BODY WHEN DOING OUR INITIAL INTRODUCTIONS BEFORE THE RECYCLING PROCESS."

"SO MS. MCGEE, I HAVE ALREADY DETERMINED THAT PARKING CARS IS PROBABLY NOT THE BEST USE FOR YOU HERE AT THE ETERNITY. SO TELL ME..."

"WHAT ARE YOU GOOD AT?"

"OR...WHAT ARE YOU GOOD FOR?"

"THERE YOU ARE YOU DOUBLE CROSSER!"

"YOU'RE NOT GETTING AWAY WITH THIS."

"I'M NOT BEING TURNED INTO SOME PIECE OF ASS THAT YOU CAN PUT ON DISPLAY IN YOUR DAMN CASINO."

"I HAVE RIGHTS GOD DAMN IT!"

"WE HAD A DEAL..."

TAP TAP TAP

WHAT THE HELL?

THAT'S MY LINE DANICA!

WHAT THE HELL IS THIS?

"LOOKS LIKE A HOT PIECE OF TAIL TO ME. NICE TO SEE YOU AGAIN SAM."

"SHUT YOUR HOLE, SAM! DON'T YOU DARE RAISE YOUR VOICE TO ME OR ANYONE ELSE AGAIN FOR THE REST OF TIME!"

"WHAT AM I DOING IN THIS BODY? I DIDN'T SELL YOU MY SOUL TO BE TURNED INTO SOME FLOOZY! I WANT SOME ANSWERS AND I WANT THEM NOW!"

"JUST BECAUSE YOU LOOP-HOLED YOURSELF OUT OF AN ETERNITY OF DAMNATION DOESN'T MEAN YOU'VE EARNED A WHITE ROBE WITH WINGS EITHER."

"GETTING YOURSELF OUT OF HELL DOESN'T MEAN YOU ESCAPED THE SUFFERING."

"WE KNOW HOW TO DEAL WITH PEDOPHILES AND CHILD KILLERS LIKE YOU."

"GET HER OUT OF HERE."

"SCUMBAG."

"YOU'VE GOT TO BE KIDDING."

TAP TAP

"WHY IS EVERYONE TAPPING..."

"...ME?"

"BEING A LITTLE ROUGH ON THE GIRL AREN'T YOU? SHE LOOKS LIKE SHE COULD BE FUN TO HAVE AROUND."

"JESUS!"

NEXT ISSUE:
Danica's Origin, Vintage Wine & Original Sin

Epilogue...

There's a little something that people talk about around here. It's something everyone hopes to get just a little taste of so that they can maybe break even before gong home.

It's called luck, and it's a rare commodity.

"SORRY ABOUT THE CAMERA. THESE ARE ON THE HOUSE."

"THAT WAS A FIVE HUNDRED DOLLAR CAMERA! YOU THINK A PAIR OF TICKETS TO SOME NUDIE SHOW IS GOING TO REPLACE THAT?"

"LOOK. I APOLOGIZED FOR YOUR CAMERA. THERE'S NOTHING THAT CAN BE DONE ABOUT IT."

"SO WHY DON'T YOU TAKE YOUR TICKETS AND WALK THE CASINO AND FIND THE HOTTEST LITTLE PIECE OF TAIL YOU CAN IMAGINE AND OFFER TO TAKE HER TO THE SHOW.."

In Vegas, everything turns on the roll of the dice, the flip of a card or the spin of a wheel. Everything is luck... bad or otherwise.

"THIS COULD TURN OUT TO BE YOUR LUCKY DAY. AFTER ALL..."

"THERE'S MORE THAN ONE WAY TO GET LUCKY IN VEGAS."

"Getting lucky" is in interesting term.

And everyone has their own interpretation of what it means.

Getting lucky is not always easy. But maybe in this town it's just a little easier than usual.

HI...

In Vegas, you can meet Lady Luck at almost any corner.

I HEAR YOU HAVE SHOW TICKETS. CAN I COME?

When you find her, run with her. Don't let go.

She can make you the happiest guy or gal on Earth. Money, fame sex...the possibilities are endless.

But as many have learned, you have to be careful when Lady Luck is at your side. She is a cruel Mistress.

THANKS FOR THE RIDE BABY...

...BUT THIS IS WHERE I GET OFF!

Luck can turn on you in an instant. Bad to good. Good to bad. Bad to worse.

You've got to know when to fold and go home, or she may just take you for everything you've got.

Writer: **Tom Hutchison** Artist: **Edson Novais** Colors: **Alzir Alves** Letters **Oren Kramek**

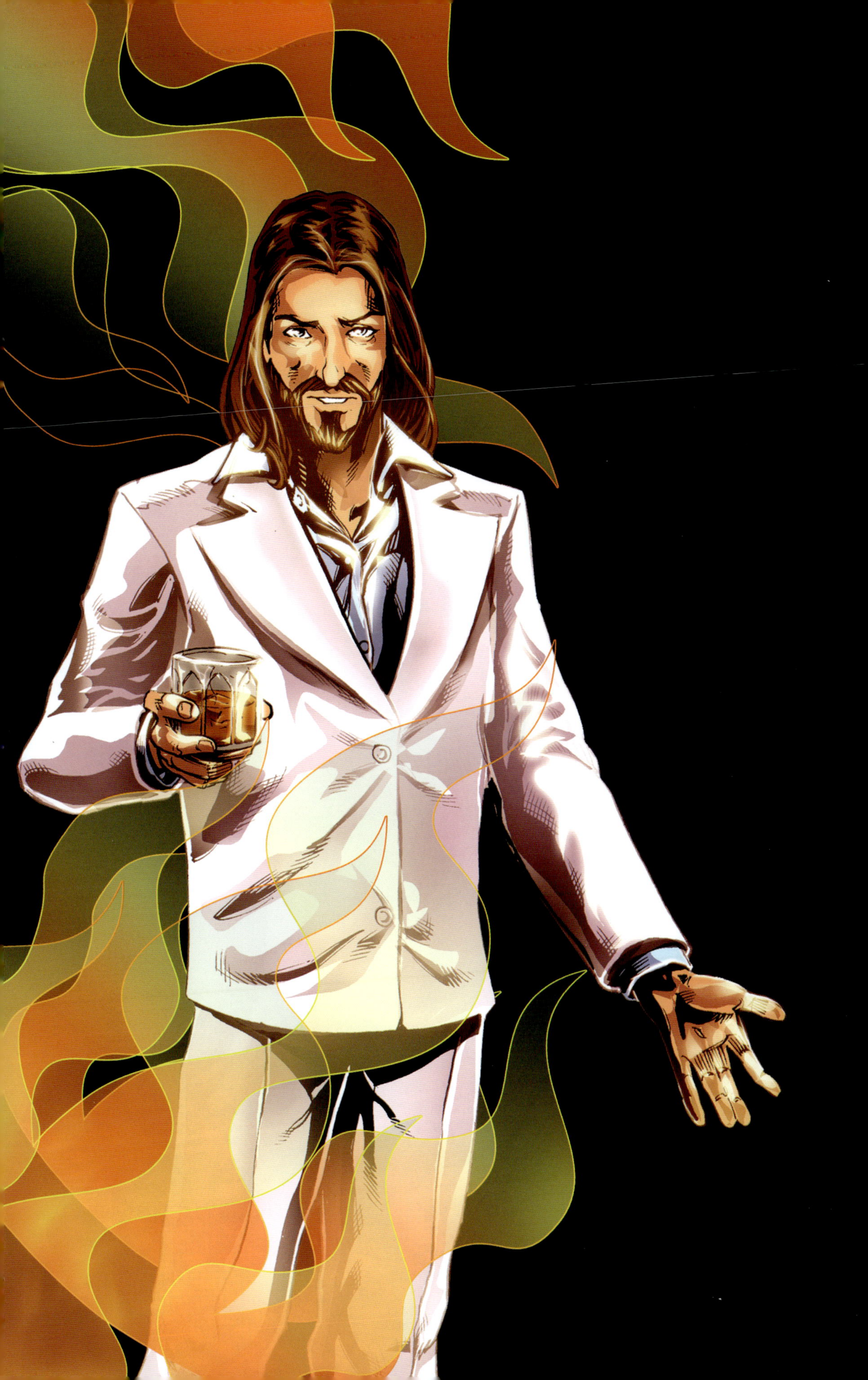

SELL YOUR SOUL!

$10 is fo... u...
Reward. card. All you have to do is SELL YOUR SOUL!

There's nothing like Las Vegas at night. Thousands of people streaming through your doors looking to blow their wad on the blackjack tables...

Or in some cases in their hotel rooms.

But in this place...The Eternity Hotel and Casino...there's a reason that new customers flood in night after night.

And she is the reason. Well I suppose it's actually her marketing strategy. When your Sire happens to be the Devil's first born son, you apparently get quite the devious little mind to go along with a smokin' hot body.

And I don't just mean smokin' hot in her outward appearance. Trust me when I tell you...she's en fuego!

Anyway, I'm sure you want to hear about this brilliant plan of hers to keep this place full night after night. Truth is she offers to buy their immortal souls for ten thousand dollars.

A pittance to some, a fortune to others.

What's your soul worth to you?

JESUS CHRIST. WHAT ARE YOU DOING HERE?
I ALREADY KICKED OUT YOUR OPPOSITE LAST NIGHT FOR BARGING IN HERE AND SCARING THE PANTS OFF MY CUSTOMERS.
DANICA MY CHILD, I HAVE NO INTENTION OF DISRUPTING YOUR GUESTS.
HOWEVER, I AM CONCERNED ABOUT HOW YOU ARE RUNNING YOUR SO-CALLED BUSINESS. I THINK WE NEED TO HAVE A LITTLE TALK.
I TALKED WITH MY FATHER ABOUT THAT VERY SAME SUBJECT LAST NIGHT RIGHT BEFORE I HAD HIM THROWN OUT OF MY OFFICE.
YOU MIGHT BE ABLE TO WALK ON WATER, BUT I DON'T REMEMBER FLYING BEING ONE OF YOUR HOLY GIFTS.
DEAR GIRL...
ARE YOU THREATENING ME?
DING!
NNER!
JACKPOT!!
DING!
DING!
DING!
DING!
DING!
SAVED BY THE BELL BIG J.
THIS ISN'T OVER DANICA. YOU WILL HAVE TO ANSWER FOR WHAT YOU'RE DOING HERE.
I ANSWER TO NO ONE, JESUS. EVEN HE WILL LEARN THAT ONE OF THESE DAYS. NOW GET OUT OF MY SIGHT.
QUITE THE HIGH AND MIGHTY ATTITUDE HUH BOYS?
SHE NEEDS SOMEONE TO PUT HER IN HER PLACE, SIR.
IS THAT SO?

"MARY?"

"I BELIEVE YOU WERE ASKED BY THE OWNER OF THIS ESTABLISHMENT TO GET THE HELL OUT OF HERE."

"IT'S GOOD TO SEE YOU AGAIN."

"I'M SURE. YOU THINK YOU CAN JUST COME IN HERE AND I'LL RUN INTO YOUR ARMS OR SOMETHING? I WANT YOU OUT OF HERE RIGHT NOW. IF YOU DON'T HAVE BUSINESS WITH DANICA THEN WE'RE NOT INTERESTED IN WHAT YOU HAVE TO SAY."

"MARY..."

"I'VE MISSED YOU."

"BULLSHIT! VEGAS IS FILLED WITH WHORES. GO FIND YOURSELF ANOTHER ONE."

UM...

MY CHILDREN, PAY NO ATTENTION TO THE MISGIVINGS OF A SPURNED HARLOT. SHE IS WELCOMED INTO MY FLOCK AS ARE ALL OF YOU. I WILL BE DOING A LIVE REMOTE OF MY RADIO SHOW THURSDAY AFTERNOON AT THE PALACE AND YOU ARE ALL INVITED TO ATTEND AND BE BLESSED BY THE HOLY LIGHT THAT WILL SHINE UPON YOU.

HUH?

BLASPHEMERS.

LET'S GO.

NO RAPTURE FOR YOU!

HELLO GENTLEMEN.
WOULD YOU BE INTERESTED IN SEEING A FREE SHOW THIS EVENING?
OUT OF MY WAY SINNERS.
THE MESSIAH IS NOT INTERESTED IN YOUR TIMESHARES.
WELL... I GUESS DYING FOR THE WORLD'S SINS CAN GIVE YOU A BIT OF A HIGH AND MIGHTY ATTITUDE.
ADAM
EVE
DON'T JUDGE LEST YE BE JUDGED MY SWEET.
WE DID GET JUDGED, ADAM. WE LOST...
MAYBE SO, BUT DANICA SAYS WE WILL ALL HAVE OUR CHANCE AT REDEMPTION ONE DAY.
I'M NOT SO SURE I EVEN CARE ABOUT THAT ANYMORE. I LIKE IT HERE AND I DOUBT EVEN HEAVEN COULD BE AS MUCH FUN AS THE ETERNITY.

I'll be fine.

You ok?

You were right though. Things going to escalate quickly. Damien may not be able to convince Lucifer that we are a problem, but Jesus can manage to put things into play much faster. With or without his father knowing...or caring.

Hey!

Ladies, ladies, ladies! Boy are you ah sight for sore eyes. How 'bout I sell my soul to ya both and ya mud wrestle each other for the rights?

Now Bill, you know you sold your pesky little soul to me when we opened this place and you blew your money on those angels you couldn't keep your hands off of.

But that was years ago honey. I still remember you tellin' me I'd get my shot at you.

Sorry slick, one time offer and you chose the cherubs instead of the siren.

Why does Hilary let him roam around by himself?

Ha ha ha! Let's get a drink Maggie.

Make it a double.

THUMP! THUMP!

"A good choice father. What vintage?"

"It's been too long since we've had a drink together, Damien. With all the time you spend prowling up above I'm glad you can still appreciate a good wine. Can you not taste the distinct Roman flavor?"

"Of course. I should have caught it right away. Good old Caligula. Still have him on tap do you?"

"He's not replenishing as fast as he used to so I only bring him out for special occasions."

"Finish your drink and I'll take you to the wine cellar. I've done some remodeling that I think you will find most appealing."

"Walk with me."

"I HAVE KEPT THIS PLACE STOCKED WITH NOTHING BUT THE FINEST FOR MILLENNIA. I'VE CREATED QUITE THE COLLECTION, WOULDN'T YOU SAY?"

"IMPRESSIVE TO SAY THE LEAST, FATHER. WHICH IS WHY NEED TO DISCUSS MY DAUGHTER..."

VERY WELL. TELL ME ABOUT THIS ERRANT SPAWN OF YOURS.

"SO YOUR MOM ISN'T REALLY A GOAT LIKE DAMIEN ELUDED TO THE OTHER NIGHT...IS SHE?"

"DANICA?"

"I HAVE NO IDEA WHAT YOU'RE TALKING ABOUT."

"EARTH TO DANICA. GET YOUR MIND OUT OF THE WAITRESS'S PANTIES PLEASE. YOU'RE AS BAD AS YOUR FATHER."

"ANYWAY, TO ANSWER YOUR QUESTION..."

"OH SO YOU WERE PAYING ATTENTION. IMAGINE MY SURPRISE."

"I WAS BORN ON A SHIP IN INTERNATIONAL WATERS. MY MOTHER WASN'T FOUND ON BOARD DESPITE A SEARCH, THAT I'M TOLD WAS LENGTHY. I WAS PLOPPED INTO A FOSTER CARE SYSTEM ONCE WE DOCKED IN NEW YORK AND BECAME A DE FACTO AMERICAN CITIZEN."

"I WAS ADOPTED QUICKLY BY A "NICE" RELIGIOUS COUPLE. BUT ONCE I TURNED EIGHTEEN AND LEARNED MY TRUE LINEAGE, THERE WAS NO WAY I WAS LIVING IN THAT CATHOLIC DUNGEON FOR ANOTHER DAY."

"CATHOLIC DUNGEON?"

Absolutely. Think about it Maggie. Can you think of an institution that sets itself up for problems more than a Catholic school?
Hell, any religious school really. Think about what they have them wear. Teenage girls in cute, white, thin blouses that might show a little bra and then a short skirt and knee high stockings with black strappy shoes.
Pretty hot for a supposedly religious environment don't you think?
They aren't all like that. I think your exaggerating a little. Is there a point here?
I think it's pretty obvious. The priests get all horny off the girls and then they go and find a boy who trusts them and they have this poor kid bent over the alter before he knows what's going on.
And believe me when I tell you that the priests at the school aren't the only ones noticing the girls blossoming in those outfits.

"PRETTY CYNICAL VIEW, EVEN FOR YOU."

"LIVE IT BEFORE YOU CAST YOUR DOUBTS MAGS. NOW COME ON. WE'VE GOT SOME WORK TO DO FOR TOMORROW. WE HAVE A LITTLE RALLY TO PLAN."

"VERY NICE SERVICE, BARBARA."

"HEY WAIT UP!"

"THIS IS FOR YOU."

...AND SHE'S GOT A GREAT RACK.

I SEE. SO BEYOND HER PHYSICAL ATTRIBUTES, IS THERE ANY REASON THAT I SHOULD CARE ABOUT YET ANOTHER OF YOUR BROOD WALKING THE EARTHLY PLANE?

TRUE, BUT WHY SHOULD I CARE? A FEW HUNDRED SOULS NOT IN THEIR PROPER PLACE IS HARDLY SOMETHING THE LORD OF THE UNDERWORLD SHOULD CONCERN HIMSELF WITH.

BESIDES, FROM WHAT YOU'RE SAYING HEAVEN IS ALSO BEING ROBBED, AND THERE'S NOTHING WRONG WITH THAT IN MY BOOK.

DAMN... YOUR SHOT.

YOU KNOW AS WELL AS I DO WHAT SHE'S DOING. THERE'S NO WAY YOU'VE MISSED THAT CERTAIN SOULS HAVE GONE MISSING THE LAST FEW YEARS.

I AGREE A FEW HUNDRED SOULS NOW IS INSIGNIFICANT, BUT OVER TIME, YOU'RE TALKING ABOUT A LARGE NUMBER OF OUR ARMY BEING REDIRECTED AND UNAVAILABLE FOR OUR ENDGAME.

A GOOD POINT. IT IS POSSIBLE THAT THE BREAKING OF THE SEALS NOW COULD WORK TO OUR ADVANTAGE. EVERYONE HAS THEIR SIGHTS LOCKED IN ON 2012 AS IT IS, SO WHY NOT CATCH THEM OFF GUARD?

BULLSEYE.

"BLESS YOU MY CHILD. THANK YOU FOR YOUR CALL TODAY.

AND I WANT TO THANK ALL OF YOU AGAIN FOR COMING OUT TO SEE ME.

THIS RADIO PROGRAM IS USUALLY ON EACH AND EVERY SUNDAY MORNING AS YOU KNOW, BUT I DECIDED TO BRING THE GLORY OF THE LORD TO THE PEOPLE OF LAS VEGAS ON THIS FINE THURSDAY AFTERNOON...

...SIMPLY BECAUSE I CAN.

NOW LET'S TAKE ANOTHER CALLER. WELCOME TO THE HOUR OF CHRIST...

THANK YOU FOR TAKING MY CALL. I WAS JUST WONDERING WHY EVERY TIME WE SEE YOU OR READ OF YOUR BIBLICAL ADVENTURES, THAT YOU ARE ALWAYS BRINGING MALE FOLLOWERS WITH YOU.

I MEAN THE ONLY TIME WE HEAR ABOUT YOU MAKING SOME TIME WITH A CHICK IS WITH THAT MARY MAGDALENE AND SHE WAS A PROSTITUTE WASN'T SHE? HOW MANY GOLD PIECES DID SHE COS-

A HA HA! HA HA HA! CLAP CLAP CLAP

-TIK-
-TIK-

HA HA HA! HA HA HA! NICE!

OHHHHH SNAP!

HA HA HA!

WHAT WAS THAT? WHO JUST TRIED TO PUNK ME?

WAIT A MINUTE. THAT'S IT ISN'T IT? I JUST GOT PUNKED? ASHTON YOU NUT!

COME ON ASH. I KNOW YOU'RE OUT THERE. COME ON UP HERE BUDDY!

SORRY HEY-SEUSS. NO PUNKS FOR YOU TODAY. JUST A BEVY OF BEAUTIES.

I HOPE WE AREN'T MAKING YOU UNCOMFORTABLE.

WELL, WELL, WELL. I SEE WE HAVE A GUEST STAR GRACING US WITH HER PRESENCE TODAY.

LADIES AND GENTLEMEN LET ME INTRODUCE TO YOU THE OWNER OF THE ETERNITY HOTEL AND CASINO.

CLAP CLAP CLAP

YOU'RE NOT GOING TO MAKE A MOCKERY OF THIS BROADCAST, DANICA. LEAVE NOW BEFORE I HAVE TO MAKE AN EXAMPLE OF YOU.

YOU'RE SO UPTIGHT LATELY. A HOST OF ANGELS CERTAINLY SHOULDN'T BE A BOTHER TO YOU. AND BESIDES, THIS IS PUBLIC PROPERTY AND WE ARE FREE TO GATHER AS WE WISH.

DANICA, PERHAPS YOU'D LIKE TO ANSWER SOME QUESTIONS FROM YOUR HOLY HOST TODAY?

PERHAPS YOU'D LIKE TO EXPLAIN TO THESE PEOPLE HOW YOU ARE DECEIVING YOUR PATRONS AND COERCING THEM INTO SIGNING AWAY THEIR ETERNAL SOULS TO YOU WHICH IN TURN MEANS THEY WILL NOT HAVE THE CHANCE TO SIT AT MY SIDE IN THE KINGDOM OF HEAVEN AS WAS PROMISED TO THEM.

WELL, YES WE DO OFFER TO PURCHASE THEIR SOULS FOR A RATHER NICE AMOUNT OF MONEY, AND...

OR WOULD YOU LIKE TO TALK TO THESE FINE CITIZENS ABOUT HOW YOU TAKE YOUR ACQUIRED SOULS AND PUT THEM TO WORK WITHIN THE CASINO AND HOTEL?

EXPLAIN TO THEM HOW THEY NO LONGER HAVE THE CHANCE TO BECOME ANGELS AND LIVE AN ETERNITY FILLED WITH PEACEFUL BLISS AND RELAXATION. EXPLAIN TO THEM HOW THEY WILL BE LEFT BEHIND DURING MY JUDGMENT.

Panel 1:

"YOU MAKE US SOUND LIKE A SWEAT SHOP. WHAT WE OFFER IS FAR MORE THAN SIMPLY BEING PUT TO WORK, AND FURTHERMORE..."

"HOW DO YOU ANSWER DAUGHTER OF LIES?"

"I HAVE SEEN FIRST HAND HOW YOU TURN YOUR PURCHASED SOULS INTO MAIDS FOR THE HOTEL AND WAITRESSES FOR YOUR CASINO AND EVEN WHORES TO LURE MEN INTO ADULTEROUS EXPERIENCES. YOU WOULD HAVE THEM BELIEVE THAT ANY OF THESE ETERNAL CAREERS CAN BE EQUAL TO BECOMING AN ANGEL?"

Panel 2:

"DAUGHTER OF LIES? WATCH WHERE YOU'RE THROWING THOSE STONES. IT'S TRUE THAT I CAN AND WILL EMPLOY ANY OF MY CONTRACTED SOULS TO JOBS THAT ARE NECESSARY TO CONTINUE THE GROWTH OF THE ETERNITY. I HAVE NEVER SAID OTHERWISE."

Panel 3:

"BUT YOU..."

"YOU HAVE BEEN FAR FROM HONEST ABOUT WHAT HAPPENS ONCE ONE OF YOUR FLOCK IS IN HEAVEN. YOU TELL THEM DURING THEIR TIME ON THE EARTHLY PLANE THEY CAN DEVOTE THEMSELVES TO YOU AND "EARN THEIR WINGS" SO TO SPEAK."

"BUT THAT ISN'T TRUE, IS IT?"

"THE TRUTH IS THAT GOD DID IN FACT CREATE ANGELS AND THEY ARE BEAUTIFUL CREATURES. BUT HE CREATED A FINITE AMOUNT OF THEM AND HAS NOT CREATED ANOTHER SINCE HE CREATED MAN."

"THE TRUTH IS THESE LITTLE BEAUTIES WERE ONE AND DONE. GOD LITERALLY BROKE THE MOLD."

"YOU DON'T GET A SET OF WINGS. YOU CAN'T POSSIBLY BE GIVEN A HALO. THESE GIRLS WERE CREATED WITH THOSE ENDOWMENTS AS A PART OF THEIR DESIGN."

"THOUGH I WILL ADMIT THAT YOU WILL BE GIVEN A REALLY NICE SET OF ROBES AND SANDALS."

"YOU WILL NOT CHALLENGE ME TODAY DANICA. YOU WOULD HAVE ME AND THIS CROWD BELIEVE THAT YOU HAVE ANY KNOWLEDGE OF GOD'S KINGDOM? A DAUGHTER OF DAMIEN? THE DEVIL'S GRANDDAUGHTER? HA!"

"AND YOU WOULD HAVE US BELIEVE THAT THIS IS A TRUE ANGEL? AN ACTUAL MEMBER OF GOD'S CHOIR?"

"IF IT IS ANGELS YOU WISH TO SEE TODAY DANICA, I HAVE SEVEN AT MY SERVICE. BUT BEWARE. THESE SEVEN ANGELS EACH CARRY A TRUMPET. AND ONCE THESE TRUMPETS SOUND THERE IS NO TURNING BACK."

"BRING IT."

HOLD IT YOU TWO. NO ONE IS BRINGING ANYTHING TODAY.

DANICA TAKE YOUR GIRLS AND GET OUT OF HERE OR I'LL PLACE YOU UNDER ARREST FOR DISRUPTING A PRIVATE EVENT.

YOU CAN'T DO THAT. WE HAVEN'T DONE ANYTHING WRONG.

I'M NOT GOING TO HAVE ANY ANGEL ON ANGEL ACTION IN THE MIDDLE OF THE VEGAS STRIP. NOT GOOD FOR ANYONE, ESPECIALLY THE TWO OF YOU. IT WILL BE ALL OVER THAT YOUTUBE IN MINUTES.

IT'S

AND I'M NOT GOING TO GIVE YOU THE CHANCE.

MR. MAYOR, I BELIEVE I HOLD A CONTRACT SIGNED BY YOU...

I'M NOT DEAD YET HONEY, AND UNTIL I AM I RUN THIS CITY, NOT YOU.

WELL SAID MR. MAYOR.

DON'T GET SNAPPY PARTNER. JUST GO MAKE YOUR ANNOUNCEMENT AND LET'S WRAP THIS PUBLIC RELATIONS NIGHTMARE UP.

LADIES AND GENTLEMEN. I APOLOGIZE FOR THE DISRUPTION, BUT I HAVE WONDERFUL NEWS.

AS OF TODAY I AM PARTNERING MYSELF WITH THE PALACE HOTEL AND CASINO AND WILL BE STAYING IN TOWN TO KEEP A WATCHFUL EYE ON ALL WHO TRAVEL THROUGH THIS EXCITING CITY.

WHY WOULD JESUS BE WILLING TO MOVE HIMSELF OUT HERE JUST TO WATCH A BUNCH OF TOURISTS COME AND GO?

I LOOK FORWARD TO OVERSEEING THE FLOCK THAT COMES TO LAS VEGAS WITH GREAT ANTICIPATION.

THIS IS AN EXCITING DAY FOR US ALL AND I WILL DO MY VERY BEST TO HELP EACH OF YOU REACH THE DAY OF JUDGMENT WHEN YOU WILL BE LIFTED OUT OF THIS WORLD AND TRANSPORTED TO THE KINGDOM OF HEAVEN.

CLAP CLAP CLAP

WHAT'S THIS ABOUT? WHY IS HE HERE, AND BEYOND THAT...WHY IS HE STAYING?

IT'S A FREE COUNTRY, DANICA. HE CAN COME AND GO AS HE PLEASES. AND JUST LIKE YOU, HE CAN MAKE DEALS WITH WHOMEVER HE PLEASES.

SO THAT'S IT HUH? HE'S MADE A DEAL WITH YOU? YOU TRYING TO SWITCH SIDES ON ME MAYOR? MAYBE HE'S GIVEN YOU A LITTLE BIT OF WHAT HE GAVE CARTAPHILUS? LIVE FOREVER OR UNTIL HE COMES BACK TO JUDGE...

WAIT A MINUTE! THAT'S WHAT'S HAPPENING ISN'T IT? HE'S HERE TO JUDGE THESE PEOPLE!

AHHHH!

WHAT IS IT YOU'RE HOLLERING ABOUT MY DEAR?

YOU HAVE THE RIGHT TO REMAIN SILENT...

WHAT WAS THAT FOR?

YOU CAN PLAY YOUR SHEEP HOWEVER YOU WANT, BUT YOU'RE NOT FOOLING ME.

WHAT IS THIS?

I DON'T KNOW WHA—

YOU'RE HERE FOR THE RAPTURE!

MY GOD! ARE YOU ALRIGHT?

MA'AM YOU ARE UNDER ARREST FOR ASSAULT.

"GAZARDIEL..."

"YES MA'AM."

"TAKE THE HOST BACK TO THE HOTEL AND TELL MAGGIE WHAT'S HAPPENED."

"RIGHT AWAY."

"I'M FINE. TRUST ME I HAVE ENDURED FAR WORSE IN MY LIFETIMES."

"WELL LET'S GET YOU INSIDE AND I'LL BUY YOU A DRINK."

"BLESS YOU."

"SHE HAS ACQUIRED REAL ANGELS AFTER ALL. REMARKABLE. AND HE IS FAR TOO FULL OF HIMSELF TO BE AWARE OF MY PRESENCE."

"WITH DANICA THROWING DOWN THE GAUNTLET AS SHE HAS JESUS MAY JUST DECIDE TO BREAK THE SEALS ON HIS OWN AND WITHOUT ANY EFFORT ON MY PART."

THIS IS GOING TO BE FUN
Gambling
POKER
BLACKJA
NEXT ISSUE:
CAGED HEAT, PURRING ENGINES &
THE FIRST SEAL IS BROKEN

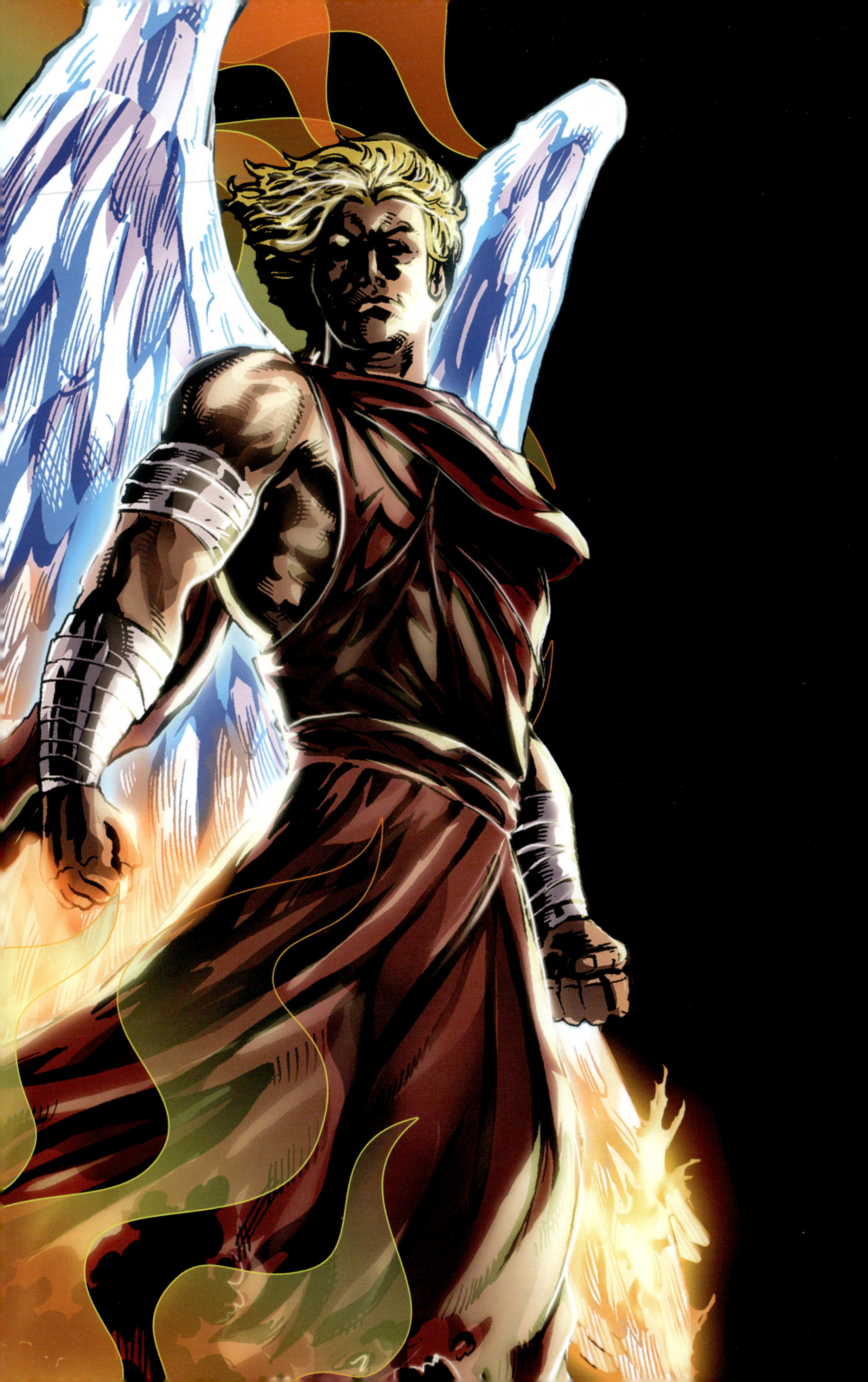

WHEEL OF FORTUNE

WOMEN'S DETENTION FACILITY. LAS VEGAS, NEVADA.

I've been handcuffed before. And I'm confident enough to admit I might have even liked it a few times. But not like this.

This is different. This is bullshit. How do I get locked up for pushing someone to the ground?

OK fine. I pushed Jesus Christ to the ground. But they are calling it "aggravated" assault because I have long finger nails that could have scratched him. Sounds a lot like the crap they pull in the NFL nowadays when a linebacker sneezes on a quarterback and gets called for a late hit. Ridiculous.

The worst part about the situation is that I could get out of here any time I wanted. Being a demon with lineage that leads straight back to Lucifer himself has certain powerful perks.

But if I break myself out, I lose. And Jesus knows it. That's why I've been rotting in this place for the last week and a half.

Of course, with my entrepreneurial spirit the experience hasn't been a total waste. Turns out buying souls in prison is a hell of a lot cheaper then at the Eternity. I bought the whole cell block for a couple cartons of cigarettes.

YOU'VE MISSED LUNCH INMATE. TWO DAYS IN A ROW...

PLEASE. THAT IS THE SORRIEST EXCUSE FOR FOOD I HAVE EVER SEEN. MAYBE NOT CIRCUS CIRCUS BUFFET BAD, BUT IT'S A CLOSE SECOND. FEEL FREE TO TAKE MY PORTION AND GAG ON IT TO YOUR HEART'S CONTENT.

"GOT QUITE A MOUTH ON YOU...

PRETTY ONE TOO. TOO BAD YOUR ATTITUDE ISN'T AS SWEET AS OUR ASS."

"YOU HAVE TO BE THE MOST STEREOTYPICAL PRISON GUARD ON THE PLANET. YOU OWN THE DVD DIRECTOR'S CUT OF CAGED HEAT OR SOMETHING?

MAYBE REFORM SCHOOL GIRLS IS AN ENTERTAINMENT STAPLE AT OFFICER HARTFORD'S RESIDENCE?"

"LET'S PUT TWENTY SECONDS ON THE CLOCK AND SEE IF I CAN FIGURE OUT JUST WHAT OFFICER HARTFORD IS ALL ABOUT. I'D SAY AVERAGE INTELLIGENCE, PROBABLY NOT A COLLEGE MAN..."

"USES HIS SIZE TO INTIMIDATE PEOPLE AROUND HIM... ESPECIALLY WOMEN."

"I'D SAY HIS MARRIAGE WAS MORE ONE OF NECESSITY RATHER THAN DESIRE AND HE STILL HAS A TENDENCY TO PROWL THE VEGAS STRIP FLASHING HIS BADGE AT THE PRETTY GIRLS, GETTING THEM TO SUBMIT TO BEING SEARCHED FOR WHATEVER HE DECIDES TO PLANT ON THEM..."

"AND LAST BUT NOT LEAST, OFFICER HARTFORD LOVES TO MAKE SURE EVERYONE KNOWS THAT HE IS IN CHARGE, AND HE'LL DO WHATEVER HE HAS TO IN ORDER TO MAKE THAT VERY, VERY CLEAR."

"SO, DID I FORGET ANYTHING?"

"YOU NEED A LESSON IN MANNERS INMATE!"

"TIME FOR YOU TO LEARN YOUR PLACE, GIRL. AND I'LL BE HAPPY TO BE YOUR TEACHER!"

"OOOF!"

"LESSON ONE: YOU WILL KEEP YOUR MOUTH SHUT AT ALL TIMES WHEN IN MY PRESENCE UNLESS TOLD OTHERWISE!"

"LESSON TWO: YOU'RE GOING TO BE HERE AS LONG AS WE WANT, SO YOU BETTER FIGURE OUT THAT THERE ARE TWO WAYS OF DOING THINGS. THE EASY WAY..."

"...OR THE HARD WAY."

"SO IT SEEMS THAT I DID FORGET SOMETHING ABOUT THE ALL POWERFUL OFFICER HARTFORD AFTER ALL."

OVER-COMPENSATE MUCH?
SO IT'S THE HARD WAY HUH?
SEEMS SO...
YOU KNOW, THEY SAY IN SPACE, NO ONE CAN HEAR YOU SCREAM...
DID YOU JUST REFERENCE ALIENSSSMMMPPH!
PAY ATTENTION. THAT'S JUST THE SET UP. 'CAUSE IN PRISON...NO ONE CARES IF YOU SCREAM.
HEY WAIT!
WHAT ARE YOU DOING?
STOP!
NOOOOOO!

YES YES YES!

YES I'LL MARRY YOU!

CONGRATULATIONS YOU TWO! AS ACTING DIRECTOR OF THE ETERNITY HOTEL AND CASINO I WOULD LIKE TO OFFER YOU A DELUXE SUITE FOR THE WEEKEND AS WELL AS A TRIP TO THE SPA FOR THE FUTURE MRS. KAVILSON AND A MASSAGE FOR MR. KAVILSON. COMPLIMENTS OF THE HOUSE.

THANK YOU SO MUCH MAGGIE. YOU CERTAINLY KNOW HOW TO MAKE PEOPLE FEEL WANTED AT THE ETERNITY.

IT'S REALLY MY PLEASURE, MR. KAVILSON.

PARDON ME MA'AM, BUT I DON'T THINK DANICA WOULD HAVE GIVEN THEM A FREE SPA OR MASSAGE, MUCH LESS A DELUXE SUITE, JUST BECAUSE THEY GOT ENGAGED HERE.

TSK TSK ELIZABETH. DANICA IS NOT HERE RIGHT NOW AND I FOR ONE BELIEVE THAT ANY MAN WHO IS WILLING TO SELL HIS SOUL SO THAT HE CAN BUY HIS GIRL A ROCK THE SIZE OF GIBRALTAR DESERVES A LITTLE REWARD.

EVEN IF SAID GIRL ISN'T MUCH MORE THAN A BLONDE HELIUM BALLOON WITH GREAT THIGHS.

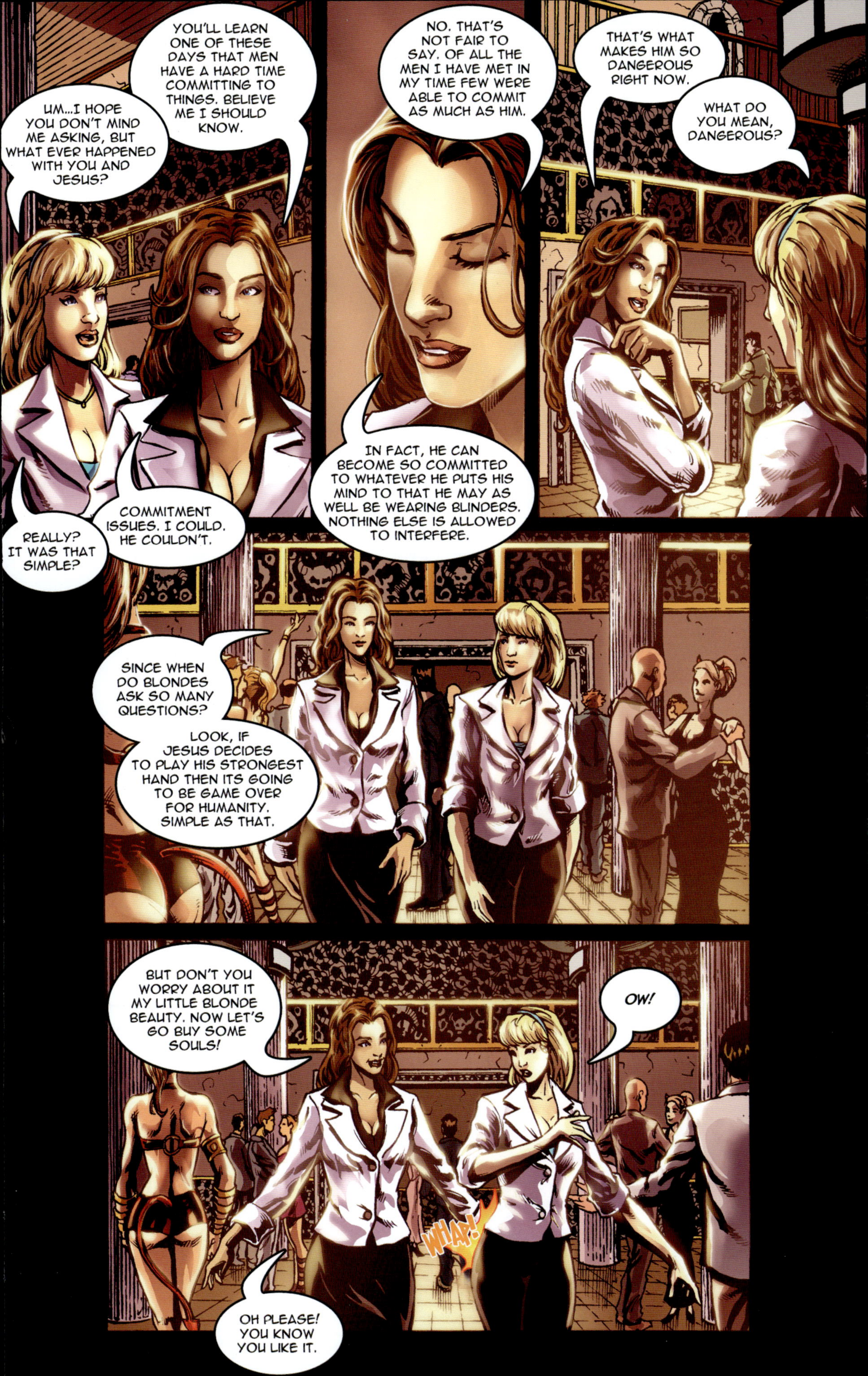
UM...I HOPE YOU DON'T MIND ME ASKING, BUT WHAT EVER HAPPENED WITH YOU AND JESUS?
YOU'LL LEARN ONE OF THESE DAYS THAT MEN HAVE A HARD TIME COMMITTING TO THINGS. BELIEVE ME I SHOULD KNOW.
REALLY? IT WAS THAT SIMPLE?
COMMITMENT ISSUES. I COULD. HE COULDN'T.
NO. THAT'S NOT FAIR TO SAY. OF ALL THE MEN I HAVE MET IN MY TIME FEW WERE ABLE TO COMMIT AS MUCH AS HIM.
IN FACT, HE CAN BECOME SO COMMITTED TO WHATEVER HE PUTS HIS MIND TO THAT HE MAY AS WELL BE WEARING BLINDERS. NOTHING ELSE IS ALLOWED TO INTERFERE.
THAT'S WHAT MAKES HIM SO DANGEROUS RIGHT NOW.
WHAT DO YOU MEAN, DANGEROUS?
SINCE WHEN DO BLONDES ASK SO MANY QUESTIONS?
LOOK, IF JESUS DECIDES TO PLAY HIS STRONGEST HAND THEN ITS GOING TO BE GAME OVER FOR HUMANITY. SIMPLE AS THAT.
BUT DON'T YOU WORRY ABOUT IT MY LITTLE BLONDE BEAUTY. NOW LET'S GO BUY SOME SOULS!
WHAP!
OW!
OH PLEASE! YOU KNOW YOU LIKE IT.

HOW DO YOU LIKE ME NOW, OFFICER HARTFORD?

STAY AWAY FROM ME! STAY AWAY!

I FIGURED AS MUCH. IT'S NOT AS MUCH FUN WHEN THE GIRL FIGHTS BACK IS IT OFFICER?

I DON'T THINK YOU'LL BE POKING ANY OF THE GIRLS IN HERE AGAIN FOR A VERY LONG TIME. ISN'T THAT RIGHT?

NO I PROMISE! I WON'T TOUCH ANYONE. JUST...

GET AWAY FROM ME!

YOU STILL DON'T GET IT DO YOU? I DON'T NEED YOUR KEYS OR YOUR PERMISSION. I CAN LEAVE THIS CELL... HELL I CAN LEAVE THIS ENTIRE COMPLEX ANY TIME I WANT TO!

I AM ONLY HERE BECAUSE HE WILL BE HERE SOONER OR LATER. HE HAS TO COME. HE HAS TO FORGIVE ME. HA HA HA!
HSSS
HSSS
HSSS
HSSS
HSSS
HSSS
I'M CERTAINLY NOT KNOWN AS BEING A PATIENT WOMAN, BUT IN THIS CASE I CAN BIDE MY TIME SINCE THE REWARD IS SO GREAT.
NOW DON'T YOU GO ANYWHERE OFFICER. I THINK MY CELLMATE MIGHT WANT TO HAVE A FEW WORDS WITH YOU TONIGHT. YOU DON'T MIND DO YOU?
N...N... N...NO MA'AM.
GOOD. MAYBE I'LL GO GET THAT LUNCH AFTER ALL. KICKING THE CRAP OUT OF PATHETIC MALE CHAUVINISTS REALLY WORKS UP MY APPETITE.

THANKS FOR COMING. HOPE TO SEE YOU AGAIN REAL SOON.
DRIVE...
YOU BETTER HOPE YOUR SOUL DOESN'T GET ASSIGNED TO ME BUDDY. I'LL BE MAKING YOU LICK THE BRAKE DUST OFF OF ALL THE ESCALADES THAT COME THROUGH HERE.
VROOOOOM!
OH.
MY.
GOD.
VROOOOM!

THIS IS A DUCATI STREETFIGHTER S WITH A FIGHTER FRAME AND TESTASTRETTA EVOLUZIONE ENGINE THAT PRODUCES EIGHTY-FIVE POUND FEET OF TORQUE AND 155 HORSEPOWER THAT'LL GET YOU FROM ZERO TO SIXTY IN LESS THAN THREE SECONDS!
AND IT PURRS LIKE A PISSED OFF ALPHA LION.
AHEM. I'M SURE. UH...SO...WELCOME TO THE ETERNITY HOTEL. ARE YOU STAYING WITH US THIS EVENING?
I'LL BE HERE FOR A WHILE, YEAH.
TELL YOU WHAT, YOU SEEM LIKE YOU KNOW A THING OR TWO ABOUT BIKES...
WHY DON'T YOU TAKE IT FOR A SPIN? I WON'T NEED IT AGAIN FOR A WHILE.
ARE YOU KIDDING?

GOD, WHAT AM I SAYING.
THANK YOU FOR THE OFFER SIR, BUT I'M REALLY NOT ALLOWED TO TAKE OFF ON JOY RIDES WITH OUR VISITOR'S DUCATI STREETFIGHTERS...
ZERO TO SIXTY IN UNDER THREE SECONDS... PURRING ALPHA LION...
AND WHY CAN'T YOU? NOBODY OWNS YOU. OR DID YOU SELL YOUR SOUL TO THIS PLACE?
UH HUH. NOW I GET IT. BUT I GOTTA SAY YOU LOOK PRETTY YOUNG TO HAVE DIED ONCE ALREADY.
AND I'D BET THAT IT WASN'T TOO LONG AFTER YOU SIGNED THAT CONTRACT THAT YOU MET WITH YOUR UNTIMELY DEMISE.
THREE WEEKS. MOTORCYCLE ACCIDENT.

"PRETTY CONVENIENT IF YOU ASK ME. YOU DO WHAT YOU LIKE MY HORNY LITTLE DEVIL. I DON'T KNOW WHO IT IS THAT BOUGHT YOUR SOUL, BUT I DO KNOW ONE THING..."

"...IF I OWNED YOUR SOUL, I SURE AS HELL WOULDN'T HAVE YOU PARKING CARS FOR ALL ETERNITY."

LAS VEGAS WOMEN'S PENITENTIARY

"DANICA! YOU HAVE A VISITOR."

"WELL LOOK WHO FINALLY DECIDED TO SHOW UP. I HAVE A BUSINESS TO RUN YOU KNOW. I CAN'T BE LOAFING AROUND IN HERE, LOCKED UP ON TRUMPED UP CHARGES FOR DAYS ON END."

"AGGRAVATED ASSAULT WILL NEVER STICK AND YOU KNOW IT. ALL YOU'RE DOING IT POSTPONING THE INEVITABLE."

"DANICA, I REALLY DON'T WANT TO ARGUE WITH YOU. I HAD SIMPLY HOPED THAT SPENDING SOME TIME HERE WOULD HELP TO CLEAR YOUR HEAD AND WOULD CONVINCE YOU THAT WHAT YOU ARE DOING IS WRONG. I NEED YOU TO UNDERSTAND THE PROBLEMS YOU ARE CAUSING FOR-"

"FOR WHO JESUS? FOR YOU? FOR YOUR DADDY? FOR LUCIFER? DO YOU REALLY THINK I CARE?"

"YOU SHOULD COUNT YOUR LUCKY STARS THAT I DECIDED TO GO INTO BUSINESS ON MY OWN AND NOT WORK FOR DAMIEN AND LUCIFER. THEN YOU'D REALLY BE UP SHITS CREEK!"

"IF YOU'RE SO SURE EVERYTHING WILL GO AS PLANNED THEN WHY DO YOU HAVE YOUR PANTIES IN A BUNCH OVER A FEW MISSING SOULS?"

"I UNDERSTAND YOUR HATE OF YOUR FATHER. BEING ABANDONED IS SOMETHING A CHILD SHOULD NEVER HAVE TO ENDURE...EVEN A DEMON CHILD. BUT THE END OF DAYS IS DRAWING NEAR."

"YOU HAVE DISCOVERED MY PURPOSE HERE IN LAS VEGAS SO I WILL ADMIT TO YOU I AM HERE TO RENDER JUDGMENT. THE RAPTURE WILL TRANSPIRE AS PROPHESIED TWO THOUSAND YEARS AGO."

"THE TRUTH IS DANICA, THOSE IN YOUR EMPLOY WILL NOT BE SAVED WHEN THE BEAST IS DEFEATED. THOSE THAT YOU USE AS YOUR STAFF, THOSE WHO ACT AS YOUR SECURITY AND THOSE THAT YOU HOLD DEAR IN YOUR HEART WILL BE CAST OUT FOREVER INTO THE LAKE OF FIRE ALONGSIDE LUCIFER AND HIS MINIONS..."

"EVEN MARY."

"I WILL BE UNABLE TO OFFER HER A CHANCE AT ETERNAL LIFE IF SHE CHOOSES TO STAY AT YOUR SIDE."

"YOU GONNA CRY ME A RIVER NOW?"

"YOU EXPECT ME TO BELIEVE THAT IN TWO THOUSAND YEARS, NOT ONCE DID YOU HAVE A CHANCE TO TAKE A TRIP DOWN TO PURGATORY TO SAVE THE WOMAN YOU CLAIM TO LOVE AND RAISE HER UP TO BE WITH YOU?"

"THAT IS THE BIGGEST PILE-OF-CRAP STORY I HAVE EVER HEARD. YOU'VE HAD TWO THOUSAND YEARS TO PULL HER OUT OF PURGATORY AND MAKE THINGS RIGHT. INSTEAD YOU LEFT HER TO ROT WITH THE REST OF YOUR CAST OFFS."

"DANICA, TIME DOES NOT MOVE THE SAME IN HEAVEN AS IT DOES ON EARTH. I NEVER HAD A CH–"

"THIS IS WHY I'M DOING WHAT I'M DOING! YOU, LUCIFER AND THE LOT OF YOU ALL PLAY GAMES WITH PEOPLE'S LIVES AND SOULS. YOU REALLY DON'T CARE ABOUT THEM AT ALL! THEY'RE JUST PIECES TO BE MOVED AROUND ON YOUR CHESS BOARD AND SACRIFICED WHEN THEY'RE OF NO FURTHER USE TO YOU!"

"ENOUGH OF THIS! I'M OUT OF HERE AND THERE'S NOTHING YOU CAN DO TO STOP ME!"

"YOU'RE NOT GOING ANYWHERE LADY!"

HSSS HSSS HSSS

"AHHHH! SHE BURNED ME! GET SOME WATER!"

"HA HA HA!"

"DANICA WAIT, PLEASE."

"I'M DONE PLAYING YOUR GAMES."

"NO GAMES."

"PLEASE."

"I HAVE SOMETHING TO SHOW YOU."

DANICA, DAUGHTER OF DAMIEN, I HEREBY FORGIVE YOUR TRESPASSES AGAINST ME AND EQUALLY YOUR TRESPASSES AGAINST MY FATHER. YOU ARE WASHED CLEAN OF YOUR SINS AND ARE PURE IN GOD'S EYES, DESPITE YOUR LINEAGE.

MY CHILD, YOU ARE ONE OF GOD'S CREATURES. GOD CREATED LUCIFER WHO IN TURN CREATED DAMIEN...AND SO ON. YOU ARE FORGIVEN AND NOW HAVE A CHANCE TO SET THINGS RIGHT WITH WHAT YOU HAVE DONE.

WHAT?

CRICK

"WITH THE FIRST SEAL OF THE APOCALYPSE BROKEN, THE END OF DAYS WILL BEGIN."

CRACK-A-BOOOOOOOM!

"YOU HAVE AMASSED A SIZEABLE COLLECTION OF SOULS, AND MUST NOW CHOOSE YOUR SIDE."

"YOU ARE CLEANSED AND HAVE BEEN MADE AWARE OF WHAT IS COMING. YOU HAVE THE FREE WILL TO MAKE YOUR DECISIONS NOW. CHOOSE WISELY DANICA..."

"COME"

✝ "...FOR WAR IS UPON US ALL."

DID YOU HEAR SOMETHING?

YEAH THAT THUNDER WAS SUPER LOUD.

NO...NOT THE THUNDER. SOMETHING ELSE.

Something's happened...

MA'AM?

I GOT IT JOSIE.

TAKE ME HOME.

YES MA'AM.

I hope Danica is alright.

NEXT ISSUE: DEMONS ON THE LOOSE, ALLIANCES FORGED AND ANGELS GONE WILD!

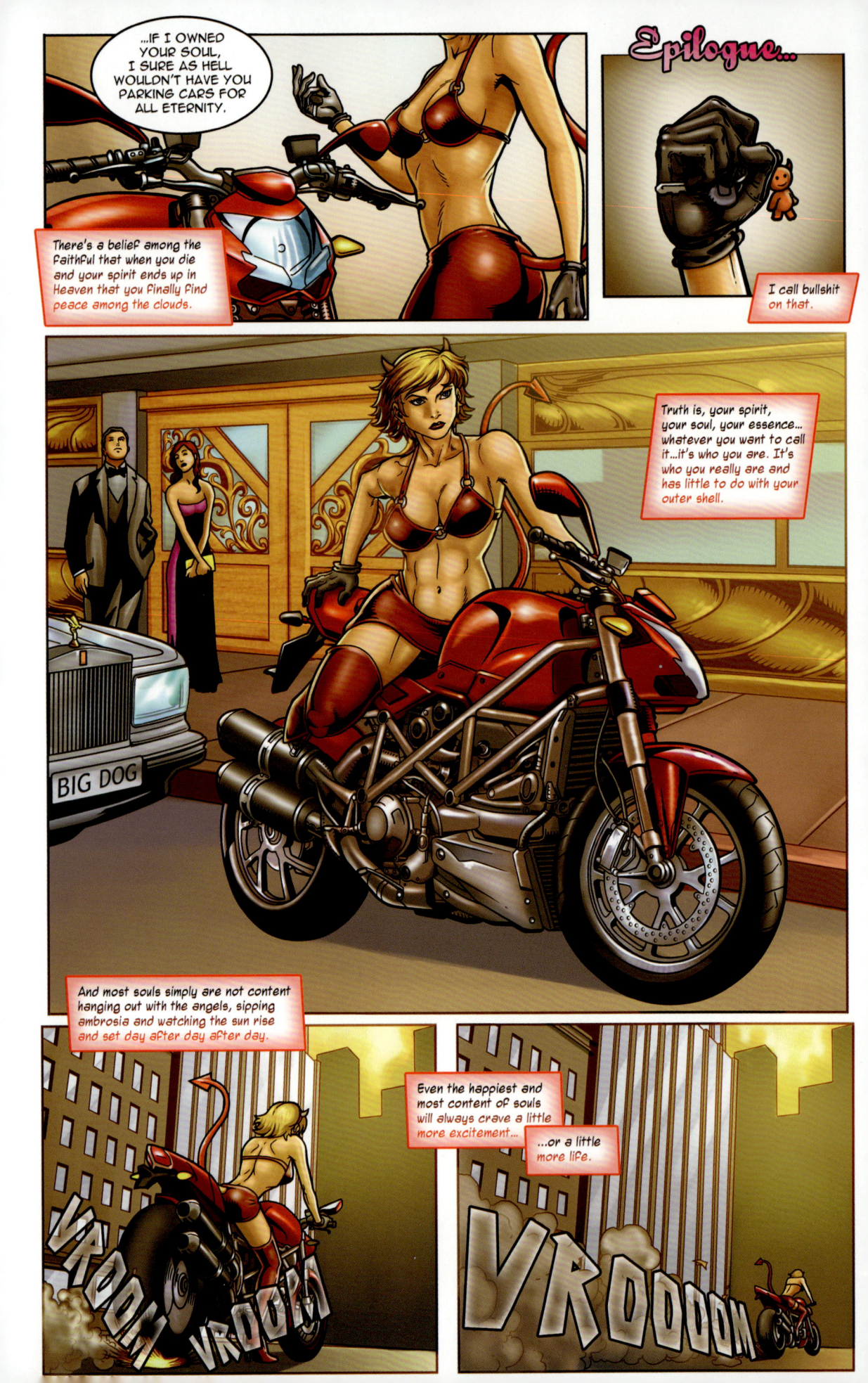

"...IF I OWNED YOUR SOUL, I SURE AS HELL WOULDN'T HAVE YOU PARKING CARS FOR ALL ETERNITY."

Epilogue...

There's a belief among the faithful that when you die and your spirit ends up in Heaven that you finally find peace among the clouds.

I call bullshit on that.

Truth is, your spirit, your soul, your essence... whatever you want to call it...it's who you are. It's who you really are and has little to do with your outer shell.

BIG DOG

And most souls simply are not content hanging out with the angels, sipping ambrosia and watching the sun rise and set day after day after day.

Even the happiest and most content of souls will always crave a little more excitement...

...or a little more life.

VROOM VROOM

VROOOM

Think about this. Even Angels get bored up in their lofty perch.

It's one of the reasons God flooded the Earth. Read the Book of Enoch if you'd like to see the details.

While certainly a better option than Hell, Heaven as it turns out is in fact quite mundane compared to the life humans get to live on Earth.

Every day for a human is potentially different from the previous one, and that extra little touch is something that most humans crave their whole lives even if they don't know it.

Because once you're upstairs, it's an eternity of Tiddley-Winks for the most part. That and getting to watch the people on Earth still having the excitement your soul craves.

And if the Angels were tempted enough to come down from Heaven and have a good time, what makes you think you should be held to a standard higher then them?

Now granted most of those Angels are what is now termed "Fallen", but the point is this...

Life on this plane can really suck, but there must be something here worth paying attention to if it attracted Angels out of Heaven's gates a couple thousand years ago.

There's always something you can be doing to make your life better, or at least more interesting.

For some it's sex, drugs and rock n' roll.

For others, it's all about someone to come home to and cozy up with.

And for the truly rare breed, an open road and a full tank of gas will do just fine.

Doesn't sound too bad to me. What did you do to make your life more interesting today?

Writer: **Tom Hutchison** Art: **Mannix** Colors: **Shi Peng Li** Letters: **Oren Kramek**

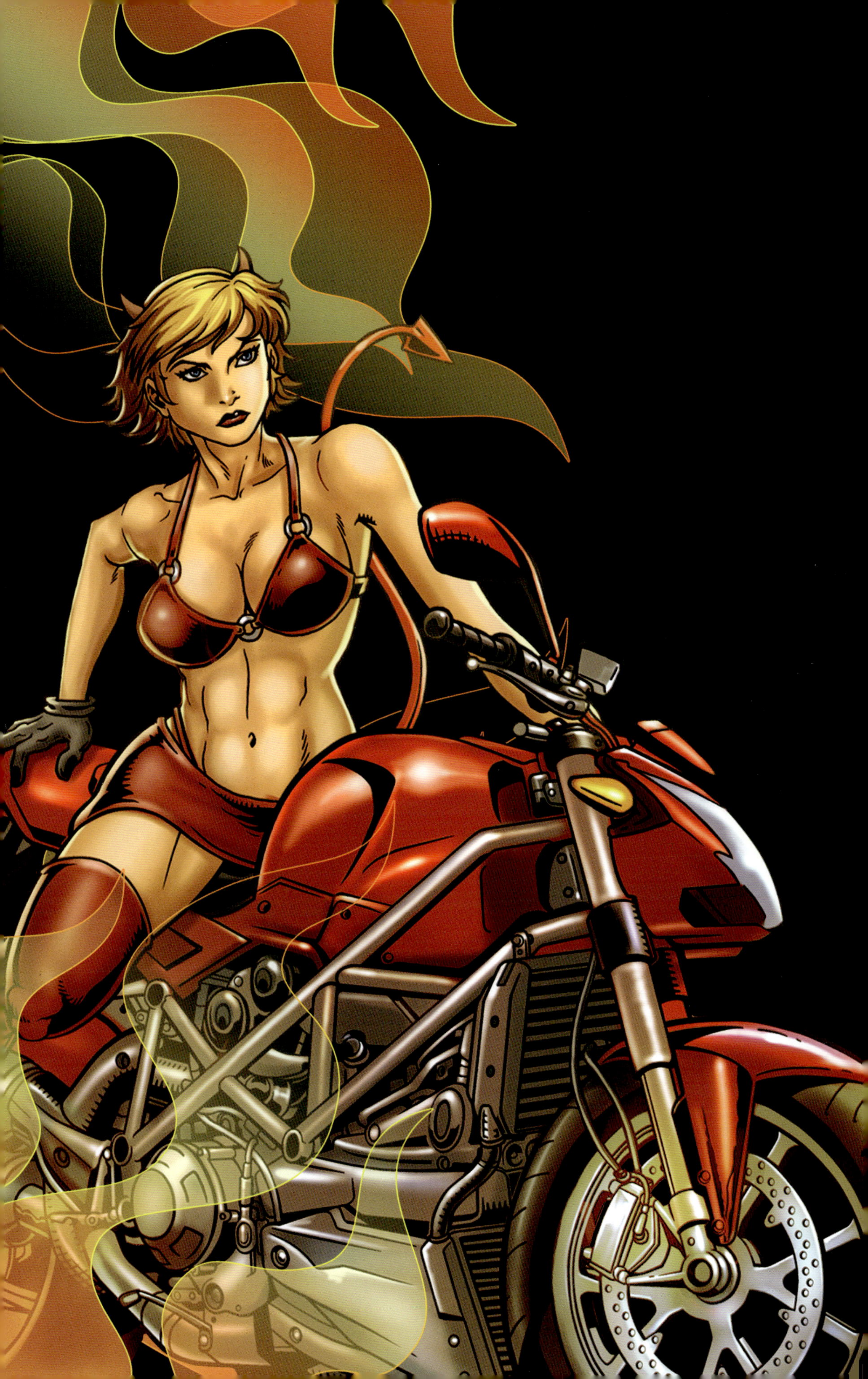

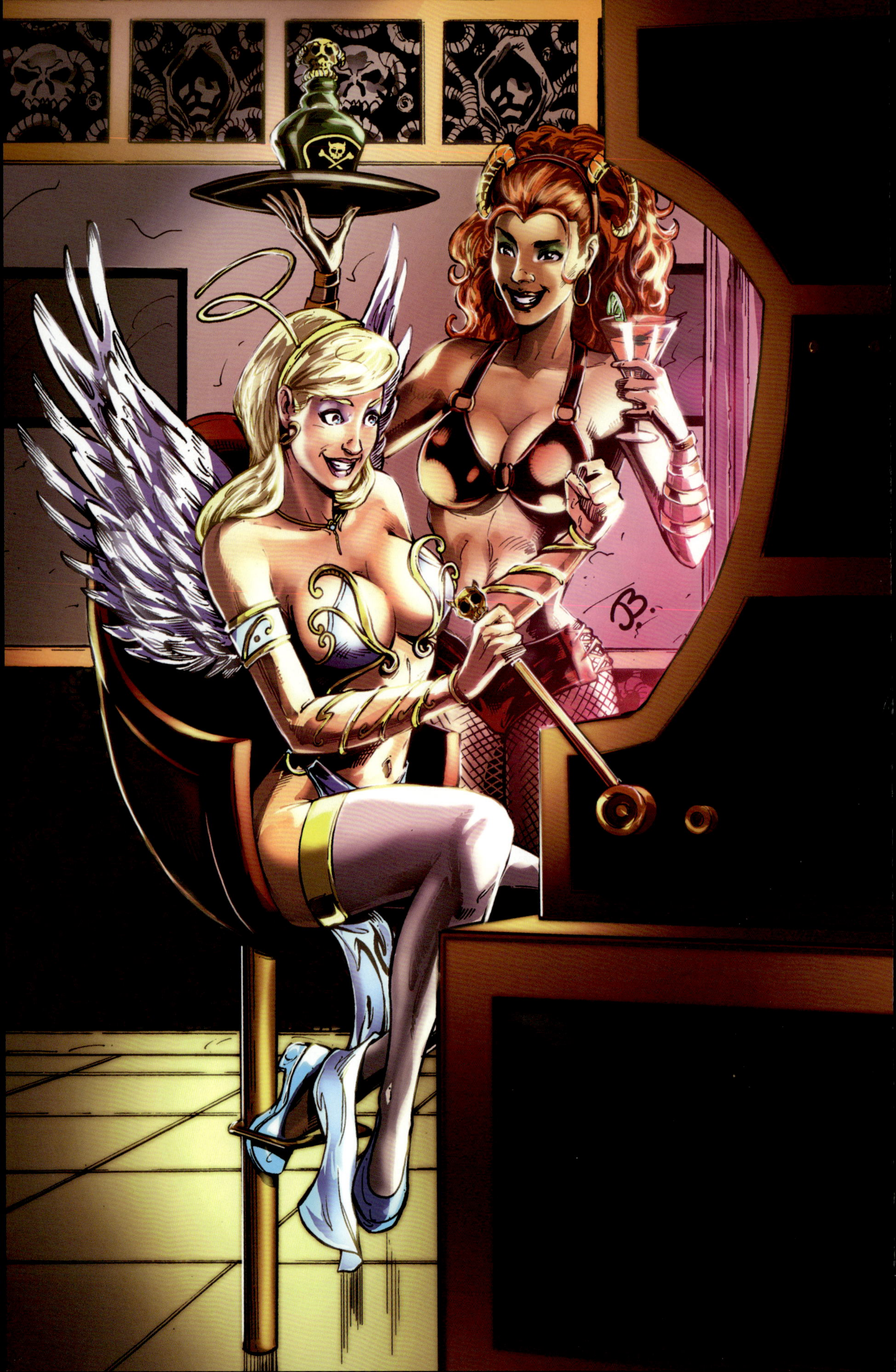

You've been so patient with me. I can't believe we've been together for so long now. Six months? Maybe more?

I never believed you'd wait this long to get a little action out of me! I know I've been a horrible tease...

I think this is going to be the night.

Really? Are you sure?

Yeah...

Do you want to head up to your room. Are you ready for me, baby?

WHAT THE HELL IS THAT?

"HUMAN TRASSSSSH! YOU THINK YOU CAN CHEAT ME, HUH?"

"OOK UT!"

I'M GONNA SSSHOW YOU HOW WE DO THINGSSS DOWNTOWN!

YOU THINK I'M SSSSTUPID OR SSSSOMETHIN' JUST 'CAUSSSSE I'M A MONSSSTER?

Nnn...NO... OF COURSE NOT!

YOU PULL A SSSTRAIGHT FLUSSSH TO THE KING WHEN I GOT THE SSSAME TO A QUEEN?

I DIDN'T DO ANYTHING!

Mmmmm! Ppphhhfff!

HELP MEEEEE!

AHHHHHHHH!!!!
HUH?
HOLY SHIT!
SIR PLEASE, WATCH THE LANGUAGE.
OH JEEZE... SORRY...MISTER... UH...ANGEL.
AH, THE BABY SSSITTERSSS ARE HERE.

"I HEAR ANGELSSS ARE FINGER LICKIN' GOOD ONCE THEY'RE PLUCKED!"

"HOLD YOUR FIRE!"

"TO BAD NONE OF YOUR FEMALESSS CAME TO HELP!"

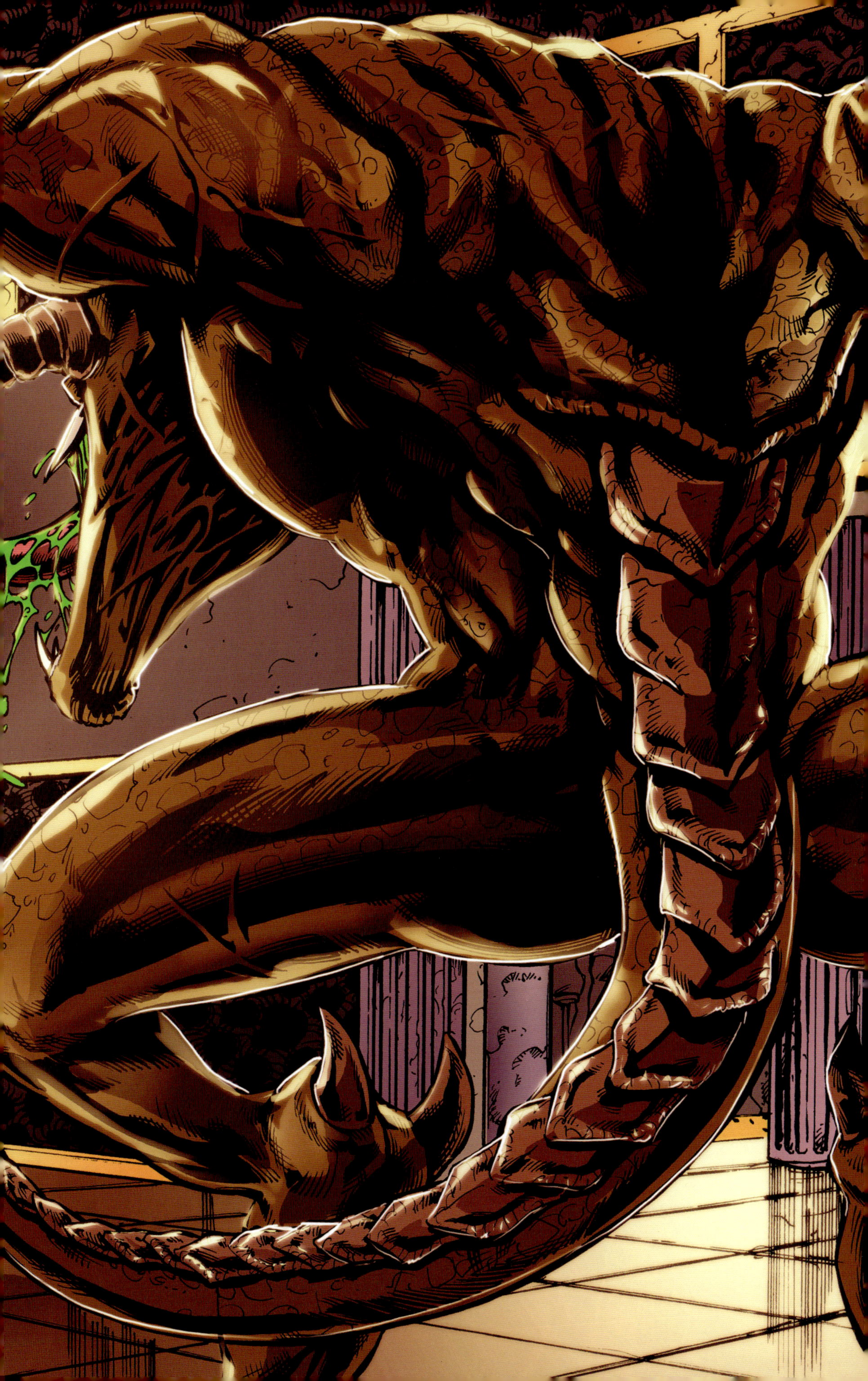

GAAACK!

WHUMP!

"NICE AIM, NEMAMIAH."

"FOLLOW ME QUICKLY."

"THIS HAS ONLY JUST BEGUN..."

WHAT THE HELL IS GOING ON HERE?

THIS WHOLE PLACE HAS GONE BATSHIT! WHO STARTED THIS MESS?

AND WHERE DID ALL THESE DEMONS COME FROM?

IT SEEMS TO HAVE STARTED WITH THE DEMON IN THE POKER ROOM ABOUT TEN MINUTES AGO.

BUT WE CAN'T CONFIRM AT THIS TIME. EVERYTHING STARTED ALMOST SIMULTANEOUSLY NOT LONG AFTER THE STORM BEGAN.

YOU GUYS JUST KEEP YOUR EYES ON THIS MESS AND GET SECURITY TO HELP CLEAR THE BUILDING.

BUZZ ME WHEN YOU GET ANYTHING. I'M HEADING DOWN TO THE CASINO FLOOR.

WAIT A SECOND. WHAT'S THE STORY ON JOE COOL IN THE POKER ROOM? HOW LONG AS HE BEEN HERE AND WHY ISN'T HE FREAKING OUT LIKE THE REST OF THE CATTLE IN THIS PLACE?

I'LL VISUAL I.D. HIM AND FIND OUT.

DANICA I NEED YOU...

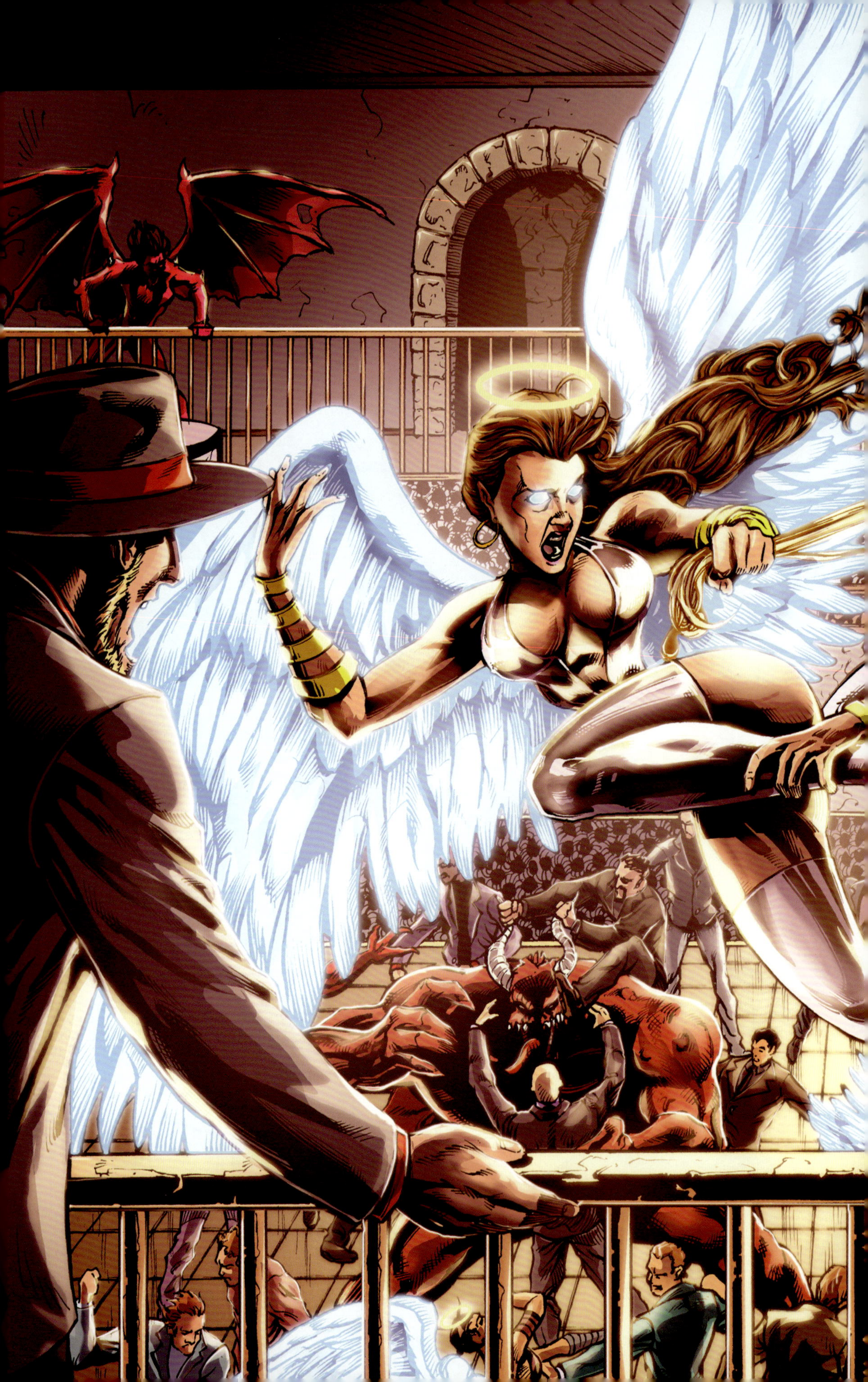

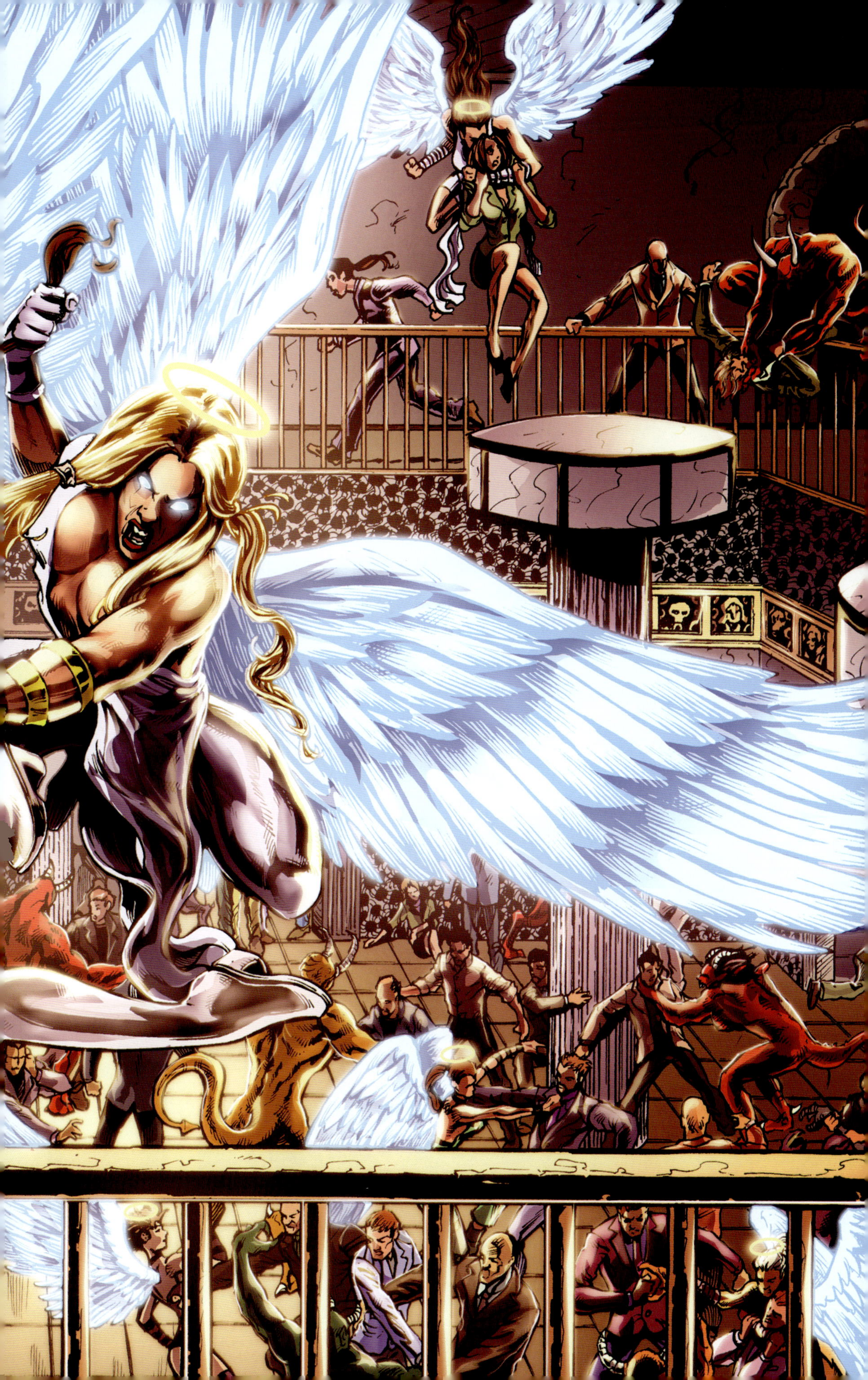

"SIR, ARE YOU ALRIGHT?"

"JUST FINE."

"WELL UNDER THE CIRCUMSTANCES WE ARE GOING TO HAVE TO CLOSE THE POKER ROOM."

"WHY DON'T YOU JOIN ME?"

"WE COULD PLAY A LITTLE GAME."

"YOU DON'T HAVE TO DO THAT. I'LL BE FINE HONEY."

"HOW DOES A LITTLE STRIP POKER SOUND?"

WHAT'S SHE DOING?
LOOKS LIKE SHE'S PLAYING CARDS.
HEY!
BASH!
AHHH!!
THIS IS A BUNCH OF CRAP! WE SHOULD BE DOWN THERE KICKING THOSE GOD DAMN DEMONS OUT OF HERE!
WHAT ARE YOU TALKING ABOUT? THERE'S NOTHING YOU CAN DO DOWN THERE!
YEAH JUST COOL IT FRANK!
YOU WANNA FIGHT FRANKIE! COME GET SOME!
OOOOFFF!

"AND THERE WENT OUT A HORSE THAT WAS RED: AND POWER WAS GIVEN TO HIM THAT SAT THEREON TO TAKE PEACE FROM THE EARTH, AND THAT THEY SHOULD KILL ONE ANOTHER: AND THERE WAS GIVEN UNTO HIM A GREAT SWORD."

SUCH POETRY.

SOUL

HIS INFLUENCE IS SPREADING QUICKLY. IT WON'T BE LONG BEFORE THIS ENTIRE CITY IS WRAPPED IN A BLANKET OF HATRED AND VIOLENCE.
ONCE HE DRAWS HIS SWORD THE EARTH WILL FALL QUICKLY UNDER HIS POWER, LORD LUCIFER. WON'T JESUS STEP IN AT SOME POINT?
NO, NO XAPHAN. THE LAMB HAS RELEASED THIS HORSEMAN UPON THE WORLD, NOT I.
INTERESTING THAT HE WOULD BE WILLING TO PUT HIS FLOCK THROUGH SUCH A HORRIFIC EVENT.
IT SEEMS HE IS TAKING HIS PART IN THE GAME VERY SERIOUSLY.
I AM NEEDED ELSEWHERE. THE REST OF YOU ARE DISMISSED.
GO ENJOY THE VEGAS NIGHTLIFE!

"THIS TOWN IS ROCKIN' TONIGHT!"

"THAT'S MY GIRLFRIEND UP THERE YOU BASTARDS!"

"NICE ONE DUDE!"

"SHE'S A HOT TAMALE FOR SURE MAN! THANKS FOR SHARING!"

"SHAKE IT BABY!"

"TAKE IT OFF!"

"SCREW YOU BUDDY! YOU'RE NOT GONNA TOUCH MY GIRL!"

"YOU WANT A PIECE?"

"HEY KNOCK IT OFF YOU GUYS! THAT'S MY BOYFRIEND! LEAVE HIM ALONE!"

"DON'T HURT HIMMM!"

LORD DAMIEN?
NOT SO FAST, BERITH... YOU ANGELIC FAILURE.
I SAW HER FIRST!
SHE'S MINE, DAMIEN. I'LL NOT RELEASE HER TO YOU.

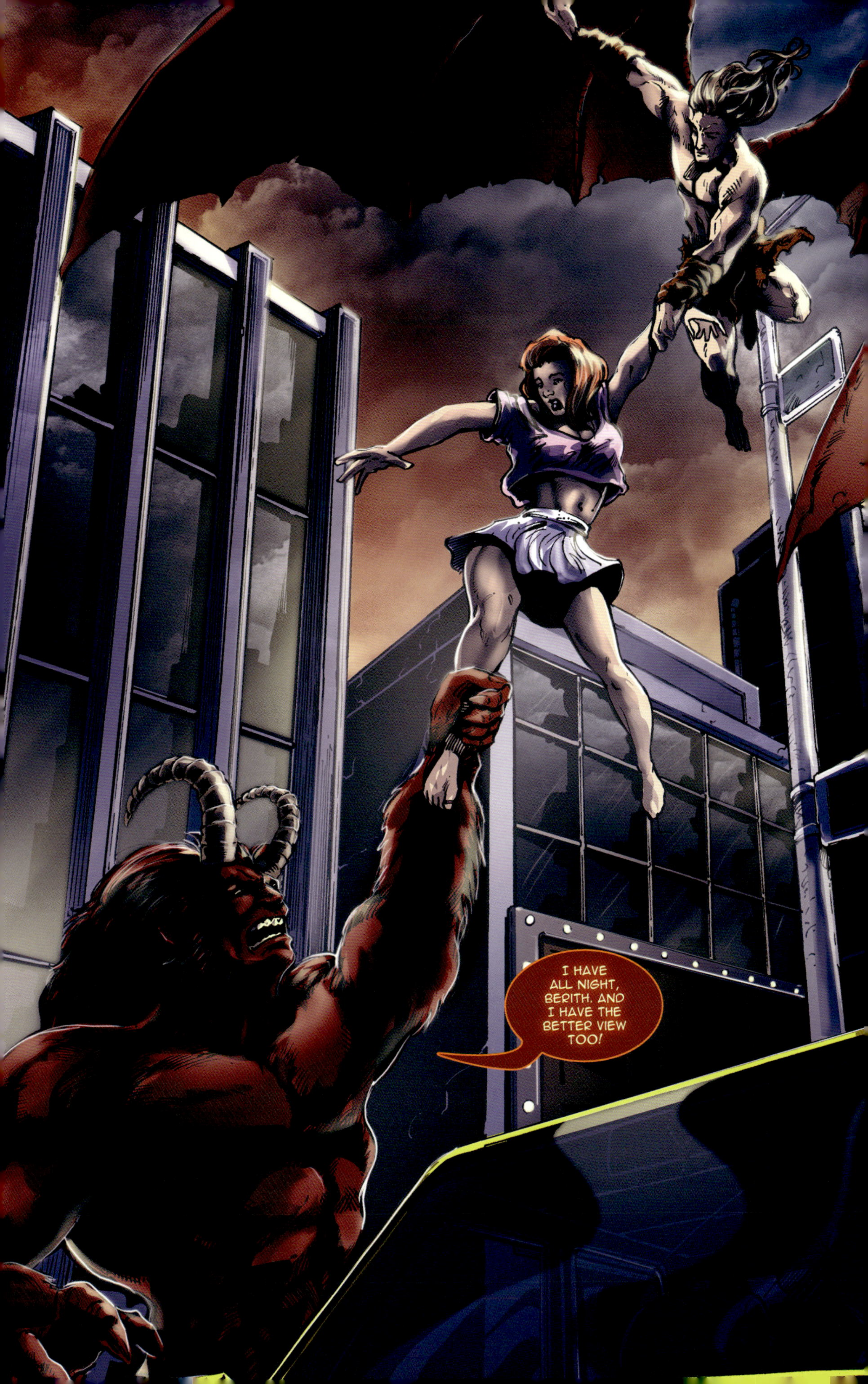
I HAVE ALL NIGHT, BERITH. AND I HAVE THE BETTER VIEW TOO!

"PLEASE DON'T LET ME GO! DON'T LET THAT THING GET ME. YOU'RE AN ANGEL RIGHT? YOU'RE SUPPOSED TO HELP PEOPLE. I'LL COME WITH YOU, I'LL DO ANYTHING YOU WANT."

"JUST DON'T LET—"

"—GO!?!?"

"NOOO!!"

"I CAN'T STAND A WOMAN WHO WHINES."

"ANGELS HAVE NO FIGHT IN THEM, GIRL. NEVER PUT YOUR FAITH IN SOMETHING THAT FALLS SO EASILY."

"MAYBE. BUT WE HAVE A LOT OF THINGS TO DO BEFORE WE GET TO THAT."

"ARE YOU GOING TO KILL ME?"

"BY THE WAY, NICE UNDIES. BUT IT'S NOT TUESDAY BABY. SO LET'S GET THESE OFF OF YOU."

"YOU'RE A REAL LADIES MAN, POP!"

"NOW PUT DOWN YOUR BIMBO. IT'S TIME WE HAD A LONG OVERDUE FATHER DAUGHTER TALK!"

NEXT: WAR

Epilogue...

There was a time not so long ago that the idea of a pair of angels fighting would have led me to images of flowing hair being pulled...

Full red lips layered with far too much lip gloss...

Soft skin and softer wings being swatted with pillows or even the sound of an occasional bare palm on a bare ass.

But I can tell you that the reality of this event is far more impressive and far more terrifying than I would ever have imagined.

An angel is wrath and fury wrapped up in a shell of beauty and grace.

To see two such beautiful creatures trying to kill each other is more than enough to make anyone doubt that there is a higher power guiding us, while at the same time the mere existence of the two combatants dictates that there must be.

Within the game that's being played out on Earth, this result was inevitable. The prophecy that was handed down two thousand years ago says war will fall across the Earth as one of the signs of the End of Days.

Trick is, War isn't supposed to be first.

But my knowledge of prophecy is only just a foothold in this nightmare. Danica was the one with the plan. She has all the answers.

Or at least I hope she does. I sure could use her right about now.

Today's the day that all changes.

These people at the Eternity are my family and I will be damned if I let anything happen to them..

I won't back down again. I will protect my family come Heaven, Hell...

...or War.

Writer: **Tom Hutchison**
Art: **Mike Vosburg**
Colors: **Shi Peng Li**
Letters: **Oren Kramek**

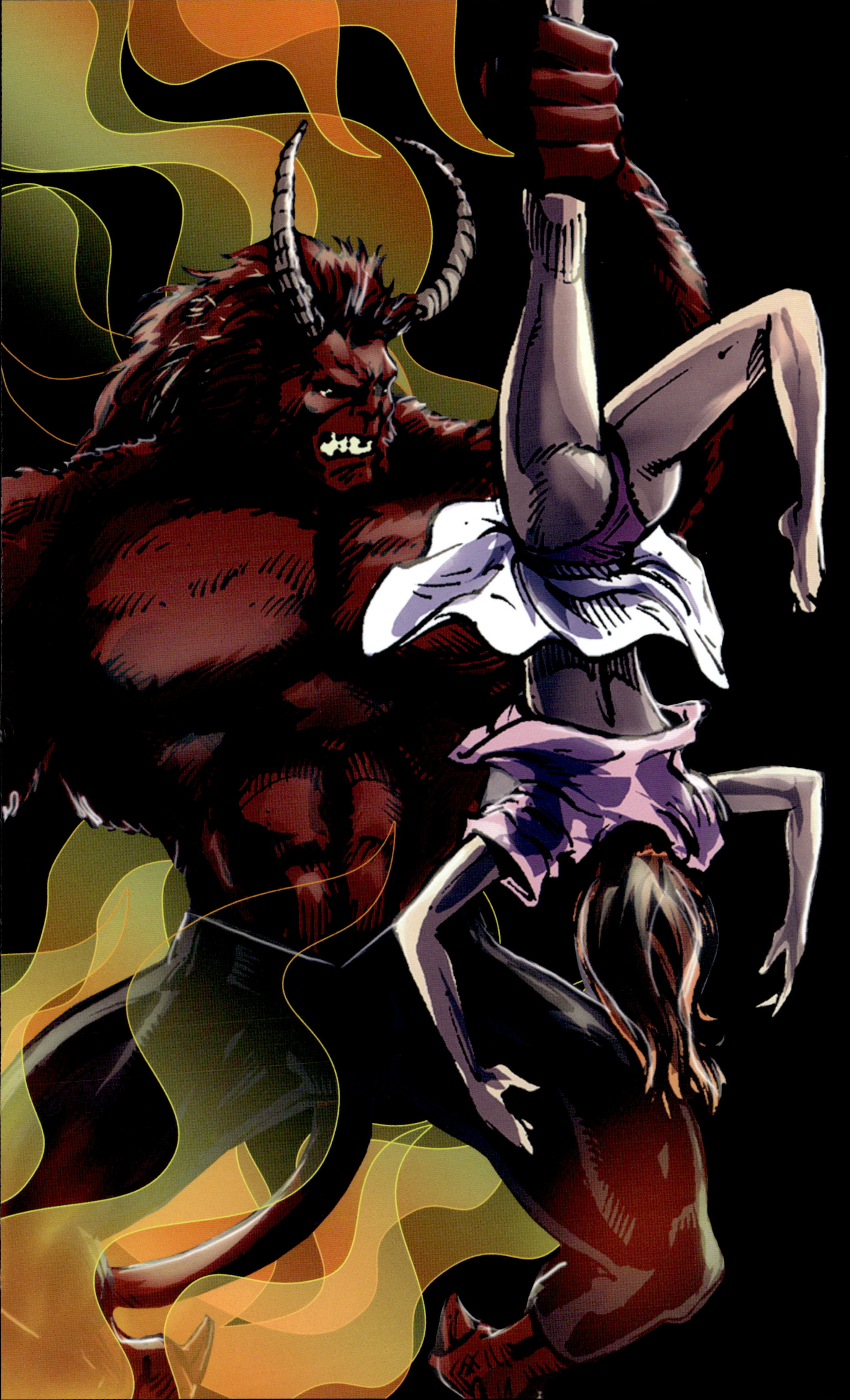

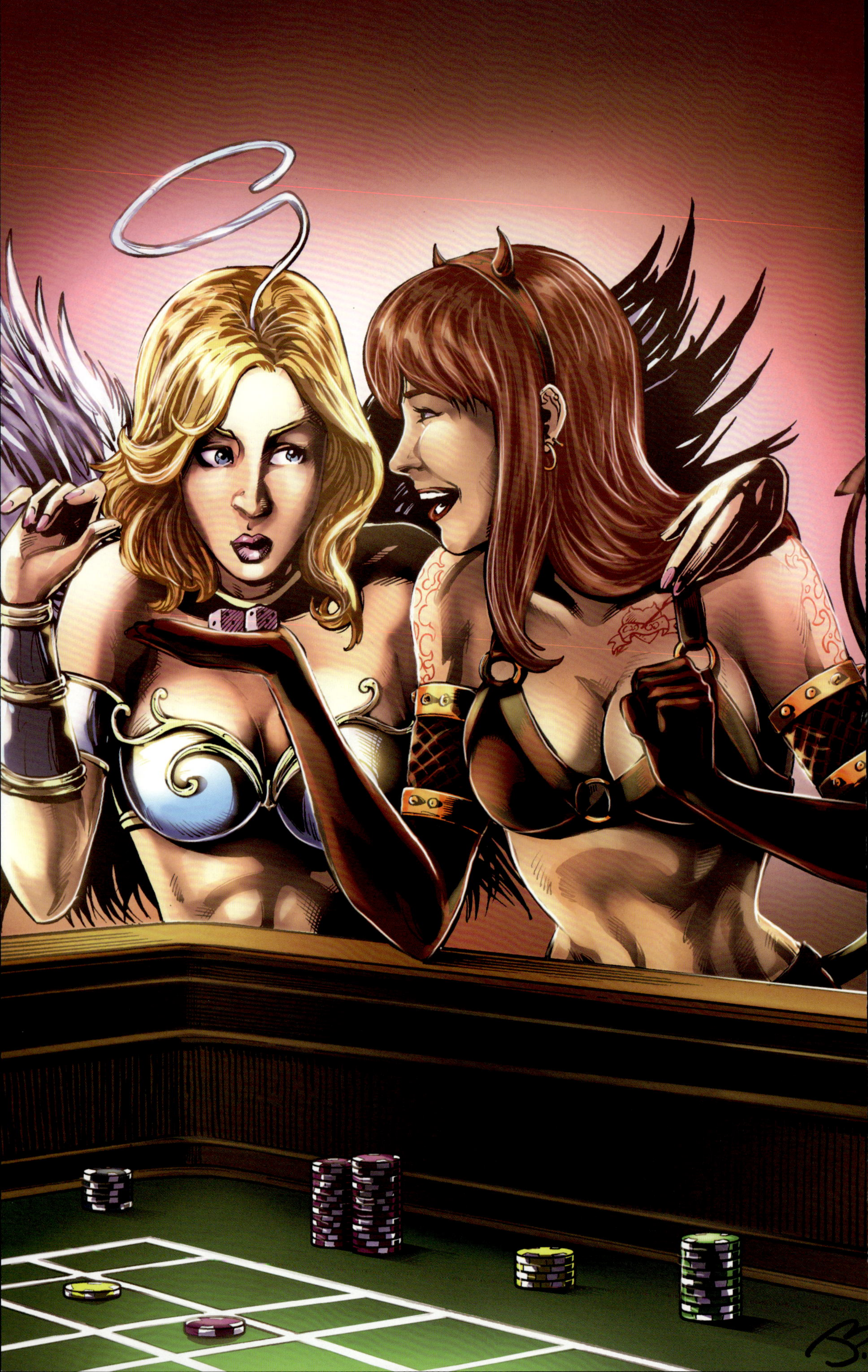

THIS IS ALBERT DESOTO COMING TO YOU LIVE!

THE LAS VEGAS STRIP IS IN TOTAL CHAOS TONIGHT. A SEEMINGLY ENDLESS FLOOD OF ANGRY CITIZENS ARE FIGHTING IN THE STREETS AND SHOCKINGLY THERE APPEARS TO BE A NUMBER OF SUPERNATURAL CREATURES MIXED INTO THE FRAY.

DEMONIC LOOKING MONSTERS AND WHAT APPEAR TO BE ANGELS ARE ATTACKING THE CROWD AND IN SOME CASES ARE BEING ATTACKED BACK.

THE WAVE OF DESTRUCTION APPEARS TO HAVE BEGUN AT THE ETERNITY HOTEL ON THE NORTH END OF THE STRIP. IN ALL MY YEARS IN BROADCASTING I HAVE NEVER SEEN ANYTHING LIKE THIS!

COULD THIS BE THE RESULT OF AN ELABORATE PROMOTION GONE WRONG?

OR COULD THIS POSSIBLY BE THE BEGINNING OF THE END OF... OOOOF!

OR COULD YOU BE ANY MORE BORING!

"YOU HAVE LET THE WORLD KNOW YOUR DOING SOMETHING CRAZY COOL AND THEY ALL HAVE TO TUNE IN!"

"YOU OLD FARTS DON'T KNOW WHAT PEOPLE WANT TO SEE. YOU GOTTA ENGAGE YOUR AUDIENCE."

"PLUS YOU HAVE TO MAKE SURE YOU LOOK HOT ON CAMERA!"

"ARE YOU READY AMERICA?"

MMMMM MMWAAAAAA!

"I KNOW WHAT YOU WANT TO SEE!"

"FEELING FRISKY TONIGHT ARE YOU? BE A GOOD GIRL OR DADDY WILL HAVE TO SPANK!"

"YOU'RE SO PATHETIC. I'M NOT SOME WEAK MINDED TRAMP YOU CAN TAKE ADVANTAGE OF, AND THAT'S ALWAYS DRIVEN YOU CRAZY."

"I WILL ADMIT TO A CERTAIN SPECIFIC INTEREST IN YOU, BUT YOU'RE GOING TO SERVE A MUCH LARGER PURPOSE THAN SIMPLY BEING ANOTHER NOTCH ON MY BELT."

"IS THAT SO? JESUS INFERRED THE SAME THING RIGHT BEFORE THEY LET ME OUT OF PRISON. NOW I'M STARTING TO WONDER WHAT IT IS YOU TWO HAVE PLANNED."

"WE" HAVE NOTHING PLANNED. THE LAMB CAN'T OFFER YOU ANY MORE THAN I CAN. SO YOU BETTER REALIZE WHO'S GOING TO BE IN CHARGE WHEN ALL OF THIS COMES TO AN END.

WHAM

OOOOF!

YOU HIT LIKE A GIRL!
IF THAT'S THE BEST YOU GOT PUMPKIN, YOU'RE IN FOR A WORLD OF HURT!
DAMN IT!
I'VE BEEN DOING THIS LONG ENOUGH TO KNOW HOW TO SET SOMEONE UP FOR THE BIG FALL, DUMBASS.
NOW I GOTTA GO FIND MAGGIE!
WELL PLAYED.

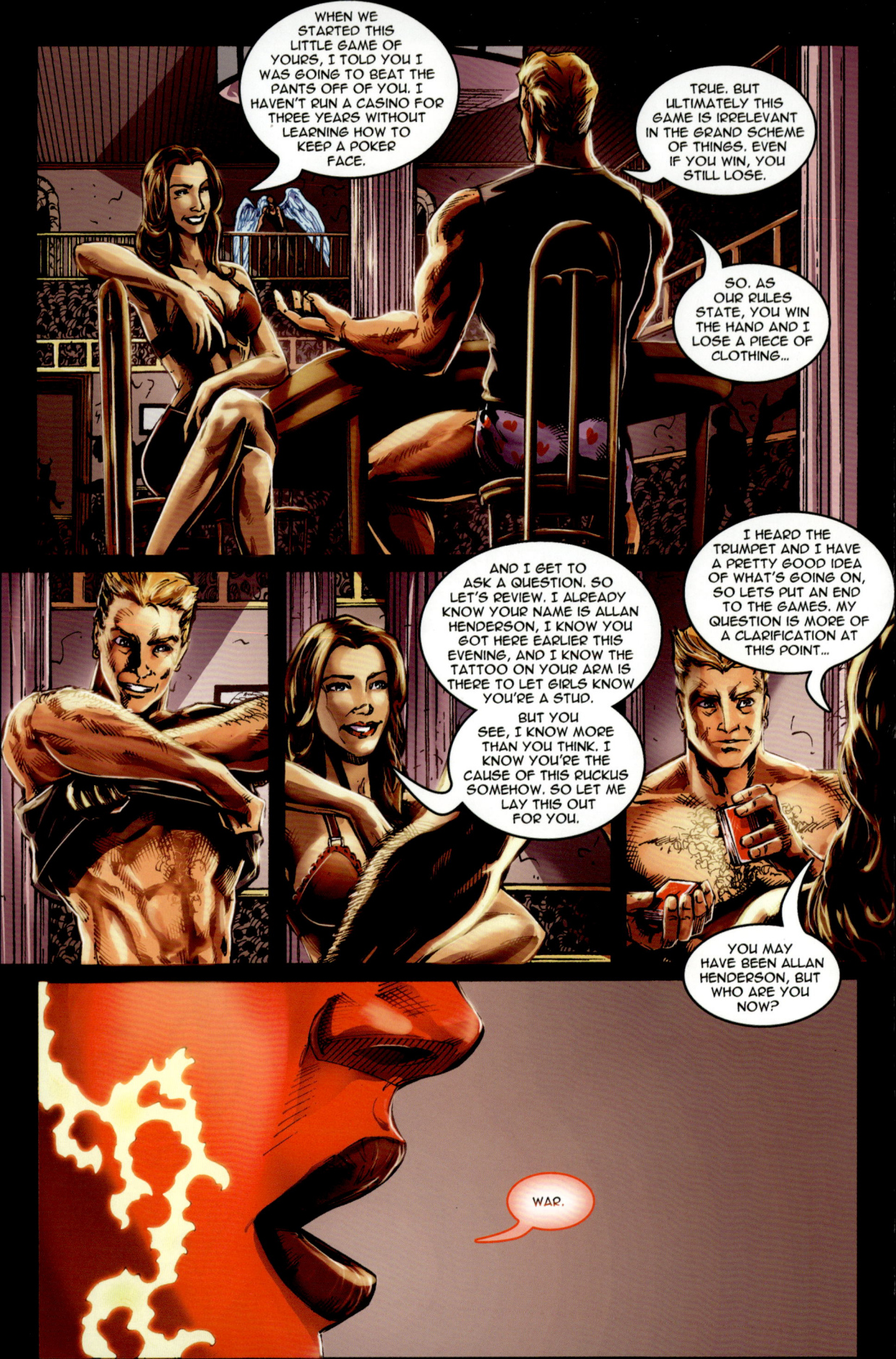

WHEN WE STARTED THIS LITTLE GAME OF YOURS, I TOLD YOU I WAS GOING TO BEAT THE PANTS OFF OF YOU. I HAVEN'T RUN A CASINO FOR THREE YEARS WITHOUT LEARNING HOW TO KEEP A POKER FACE.

TRUE. BUT ULTIMATELY THIS GAME IS IRRELEVANT IN THE GRAND SCHEME OF THINGS. EVEN IF YOU WIN, YOU STILL LOSE.

SO. AS OUR RULES STATE, YOU WIN THE HAND AND I LOSE A PIECE OF CLOTHING...

AND I GET TO ASK A QUESTION. SO LET'S REVIEW. I ALREADY KNOW YOUR NAME IS ALLAN HENDERSON, I KNOW YOU GOT HERE EARLIER THIS EVENING, AND I KNOW THE TATTOO ON YOUR ARM IS THERE TO LET GIRLS KNOW YOU'RE A STUD.

BUT YOU SEE, I KNOW MORE THAN YOU THINK. I KNOW YOU'RE THE CAUSE OF THIS RUCKUS SOMEHOW. SO LET ME LAY THIS OUT FOR YOU.

I HEARD THE TRUMPET AND I HAVE A PRETTY GOOD IDEA OF WHAT'S GOING ON, SO LETS PUT AN END TO THE GAMES. MY QUESTION IS MORE OF A CLARIFICATION AT THIS POINT...

YOU MAY HAVE BEEN ALLAN HENDERSON, BUT WHO ARE YOU NOW?

WAR.

DANICA?
I WAS WONDERING WHEN YOU'D SHOW UP.
SORRY I MISSED THE START OF THE PARTY. I RAN INTO A COUPLE PEOPLE ON MY WAY BACK FROM PRISON AND HAD SOME THINKING TO DO.
SO THIS IS REALLY WAR? HOW DO YOU KNOW?
JESUS CRACKED THE SEAL. I SAW IT.
THEN WHY AREN'T WE ACTING CRAZY LIKE THE REST OF VEGAS?
OUR WILLS ARE STRONGER THAN THE SHEEP ON THE STREETS. BUT IN TIME HIS INFLUENCE WILL SPREAD TO US AS WELL.
YOU'RE SMARTER THAN YOU LOOK, DEMON. I AM HE WHO IS CALLED WAR. I INHABIT THIS BODY MERELY BY CHANCE. IT IS SIMPLY A VESSEL USED TO CONTAIN THE SPIRIT OF MY CALLING.
MY INFLUENCE CAN ALREADY BE FELT FOR HUNDRED OF MILES IN EVERY DIRECTION AND WHEN I DRAW MY SWORD THE EARTHLY PLANE SHALL FALL INTO AN ORGY OF BLOODSHED.
THEN I HAVE MY OWN QUESTION FOR YOU, "HORSEMAN". WHERE IS YOUR MOUNT?
ARE YOU SURE YOU WANT TO FIND OUT DANICA?
TRUST ME...
YOU VALET PARKED YOUR APOCALYPTIC MOUNT AND SWORD?

"OF COURSE NOT. BUT THIS PATHETIC HUMAN I INHABIT SEEMS TO HAVE DONE JUST THAT AND WITH THE CHAOS SURROUNDING US IT LOOKS LIKE THE VALETS HAVE TAKEN THE NIGHT OFF."

"THE SPIRIT OF WAR IS CLEARLY INFLUENTIAL, BUT IT TAKES POWER TO SUSTAIN IT. ESPECIALLY TO THE DEGREE YOU BOAST ABOUT."

"DON'T TEST MY POWER YOU WORTHLESS DEMON. I HAVE MORE THAN ENOUGH POWER WITHIN ME SUSTAIN THIS FOR YEARS AND IT WILL ONLY TAKE A FEW MINUTES TO FIND MY BIKE AND DRAW THE SWORD OF—"

"EXCUSE ME..."

"WERE YOU LOOKING FOR THIS?"

"WHAT HAVE YOU DONE?"

"BUNNY? IS THAT YOU?"

THAT'S MY NAME. DON'T WEAR IT OUT!

CHILD, THE SWORD OF ARMAGEDDON IS NOT A TOY. YOU DO NOT HAVE THE PHYSICAL OR EMOTIONAL STRENGTH TO WIELD IT.
WHY? CAUSE I'M A GIRL? YOU THINK MY BOOBS ARE GONNA MAKE IT TOUGH FOR ME TO SWING A SWORD?
YOUR BREASTS ARE A DISCUSSION FOR ANOTHER TIME. BUT FOR NOW-
I THINK I'M DOING JUST FINE PARTNER.
DANICA I'M CONFUSED. I THOUGHT WAR WAS THE SECOND HORSEMAN OF THE APOCALYPSE.
YOU AND EVERYONE ELSE ON THE BIBLE BELT. ALL I KNOW IS JESUS CRACKED THE SEAL AND WAR SHOWED UP WHICH TELLS ME TWO THINGS.
FIRST, JESUS CAN PLAY HIS HAND ANY WAY HE WANTS. IN ANY ORDER AND AT ANY TIME. AND SECOND, THE PROPHECIES THAT HAVE BEEN TAUGHT FOR GENERATIONS WERE ALL INTERPRETATIONS OF THIS STORY AND IF HE CAN CHANGE THE WAY THE BOOK ENDS...
SO CAN WE.

BRAVO.

PARDON ME?

TO BE HONEST, I DIDN'T THINK YOU'D HAVE IT IN YOU.

YOU DIDN'T EVEN WAIT FOR THE ARK TO BE REVEALED.

YOU KNOW AS WELL AS I DO THAT THINGS HAVE CHANGED. IF I WAITED FOR THE ARK OF THE COVENANT TO BE REVEALED WE WOULD HAVE A MUCH LARGER MESS TO DEAL WITH.

WANT A DRINK?

I NEVER DRINK... WINE.

HOW ORIGINAL.

ORIGINALITY IS SO OVER RATED. IT'S THE DRAMA OF A THING THAT MAKES IT STAND OUT. DON'T YOU AGREE?

WHATEVER YOU SAY.

I'M IN NO MOOD FOR POINTLESS BANTER, LUCIFER.

"GET TO YOUR POINT."

IMPRESSIVE TO SAY THE LEAST. IT'S CLEAR I UNDERESTIMATED YOU.

PRETTY GOOD FOR A GIRL, HUH?

FORGET THESE PEASANTS YOU CALL FRIENDS. RELEASE ME. TAKE MY HAND. BE MY BRIDE AND WE CAN SET THE EARTH AFLAME TOGETHER!

HA HA HA! I'VE TOLD YOU THIS BODY IS MERELY A VESSEL TO CONTAIN MY SPIRIT YOU DITZ! HAVENT YOU BEEN PAYING ATTENTION?

WELL IF THAT BODY IS ALL THAT'S KEEPING YOU HERE, I CAN TAKE CARE OF THAT LITTLE PROBLEM!

YAAAAAA!

BUNNY NO!

WHAT THE HELL, DANICA?

WHAT WE NEED IS AN EXORCIST.

YOU DON'T UNDERSTAND, BUNNY. IF YOU KILL HIS EARTHLY BODY HE WILL BE FREE TO POSSES ANYONE ELSE HE LIKES... INCLUDING YOU.

"YOU PEOPLE ARE LIKE THE THREE STOOGES. CALLING DOCTOR HOWARD, DOCTOR FINE, DOCTOR HOW–"

"WHAT'S THAT SUPPOSED TO MEAN?"

"I CAN DO IT."

"IT MEANS YOU'RE ABOUT TO GET YOUR ASS KICKED RIGHT OUT OF DODGE BUDDY."

"BUNNY HOLD HIS LEGS. YOU GUYS CAN'T LET HIM THROW YOU OFF."

"MAGGIE THIS IS NO TIME TO BE TRYING NEW THINGS. WE SERIOUSLY NEED AN EXORCIST."

"TRUST ME DANICA..."

I learned from the best.

DANICA IS NO MORE BOTHERSOME TO ME THAN A GNAT IS TO AN ELEPHANT, LUCIFER. MAYBE SHE'S DISRUPTED YOUR PLANS, BUT FOR ME IT'S SIMPLY A DIFFERENT PATH THAT LEADS TO THE SAME GOAL.

SO YOU HAVE NOTHING TO SAY IN REGARDS TO THIS BUMP IN YOUR ROAD TO REVELATION?

BESIDES, IF SHE WERE TRULY A DISRUPTION TO MY PROPHECY I'M SURE YOU WOULD BE FINDING A WAY TO SWAY HER TO YOUR SIDE AND TAKE ADVANTAGE OF THE SITUATION.

BUT INSTEAD YOU'RE HERE, TRYING TO GOAD ME INTO DOING SOMETHING TO CHANGE THE COURSE OF THE EVENTS THAT ARE UNFOLDING.

A FAIR ASSESSMENT.

BUT THE ISSUE AT HAND IS THIS IS NO LONGER YOUR ORIGINAL PROPHECY. AS A MATTER OF FACT, DANICA HAS VOIDED IT BY FORCING YOU TO DO THINGS IN A DIFFERENT ORDER THAN WAS FORETOLD... BY YOU.

IRRELEVANT. AS I SAID BEFORE, THIS IS MERELY A DIFFERENT PATH THAT JOURNEYS TO THE SAME END. YOU'RE ONLY HERE TO TRY TO CHANGE THE FINAL OUTCOME OF THIS CONFLICT.

UNTRUE. ACTUALLY, I CAME HERE TO THANK YOU.

AS IT TURNS OUT, YOU HAVE UNWITTINGLY UNRAVELED THE ENDING TO YOUR OWN STORY. BY UNLEASHING WAR BEFORE YOU REVEALED THE FALSE PROPHET, YOU HAVE GIVEN ME THE OPPORTUNITY TO CHANGE THE COURSE OF EVENTS TO COME AS WELL.

"AND WHAT MAKES YOU THINK I HAVE NOT REVEALED THE FALSE PROPHET ALREADY?"

"SIMPLE..."

"IF YOU HAD, THE FIRST SCROLL WOULD NOT STILL BE INTACT!"

"THIS WAS A FUN READ, BUT IT'S LITTLE MORE THAN A CHOOSE YOUR OWN ADVENTURE STORY NOW."

"IT REALLY DOESN'T MATTER WHAT HAPPENS ANYMORE, OR IN WHAT ORDER. YOU OPENED THE GATES AND YOU'RE GOING TO SEE WHAT REAL POWER CAN DO ON THIS WORLD."

"SORRY TO RUSH OFF, MY FRIEND..."

BUT I HAVE SOMEONE I NEED TO TALK TO.

BABY, YOU DON'T HAVE THE CHOPS FOR THIS GIG. YOU DON'T EVEN HAVE YOUR PURPLE STOLE OR A BIBLE OR ANYTHING.

I'VE SEEN THIS MOVIE BEFORE. SEXORCIST RIGHT? I'M THE LUCKIEST DEMON ON THE PLANET.

SHUT YOUR MOUTH, MONSTER.

DON'T RESPOND TO HIM DANICA. STAY SILENT.

THE CEREMONIES AND TRAPPINGS OF MODERN EXORCISMS WERE ALL DERIVED FROM WHAT JESUS DID TWO THOUSAND YEARS AGO.

AND HE TAUGHT ME EVERYTHING HE KNEW.

GET OFF ME YOU THIRD LEVEL SUCCUBUS!

I MAY BE IN THE MINOR LEAGUES OF DEMONISM COMPARED TO YOU, BUT MY LINEAGE GRANTS ME THAT LITTLE BIT OF EXTRA POWER YOU'RE NOT READY FOR. AND IT'S MORE THAN ENOUGH TO KEEP YOU RIGHT HERE.

OH SHIT.

MA'AM?

BUSY HERE BUNNY. WHAT DO YOU NEED?

KEEP HIM OFF US BUNNY! WE HAVE TO GIVE MAGGIE TIME TO DO HER THING!

YOUR GRANDPA JUST SHOWED UP!

URK!

YES... KEEP ME OFF OF THEM.

ECCE CRUCEM DOMINE, FÚGITE PARTES ADVÉRSAE.

ERK! KAK!

AAAAHHHHHHH!

IF YOU PUKE ON ME SO HELP ME GOD...!

YOU DON'T SEEM TO BE WORTH MY TIME.

NOR ARE YOU WORTHY OF THIS!

OOOF!

DANICA... WHAT HAPPENED?

DON'T ASK ME. JUST FINISH YOUR EXORCISM...

And do it fast!

YOU CAN HAVE MY SWORD WHEN YOU PRY IT FROM MY COLD DEAD HANDS!

BUT EVEN IN DEATH I WILL NEVER LET GO!

NEXT ISSUE: THE END!

Epilogue...

DAMN ANGELS!

ALWAYS SO FULL OF CONVICTION AND READY TO APPEAR WHEN CALLED UPON!

BUT YOU'RE EASILY BROKEN AND ARE NO MORE THAN FIREFLIES TO ME!

IGNORANT FOWL!

NOT THIS TIME DAMIEN! TONIGHT WE PUT AN END TO YOUR ABUSE OF THESE PEOPLE!

WHUM?!

I THINK I'LL SHOW YOU WHAT REAL POWER IS LADIES...
YOU THINK YOUR GOD GIVEN POWER IS ENOUGH TO TAME ME? YOU BELIEVE YOUR PRETTY LITTLE HALOS ARE GOING TO KEEP YOU SAFE?
CRIK
NOOO! ARGH!
PLEASE DON'T HURT HIM!
WE CONCEDE YOUR POWER, DAMIEN. WE SURRENDER.
AS EASY AS THAT EH? YOU PROVE MY POINT SO QUICKLY, NOW PROVE YOURSELVES.
KISS EACH OTHER. DO IT NOW OR THIS ONE LOSES A WING.

TYPICAL ANGELS. FALLING RIGHT INTO LINE WHEN CHALLENGED. I HAVE NO TRUST FOR ANY OF THEIR KIND, NOT EVEN FATHER'S FALLEN.

TOO MANY TIMES HAVE I SEEN THEM ALTER THEIR OPINIONS AND ALLIANCES AT THE FLIP OF A COIN TO FALL ON THE SIDE OF POPULAR OPINION AND REMAIN STEADFAST AND GROUNDED WITH FATHER.

THEY ARE WEAK AND SOFT...

HMMM...SOFT INDEED.

MAYBE ANGELS ARE GOOD FOR SOMETHING AFTER ALL!

Writer: **Tom Hutchison** Artist: **Alisson Borges** Colors: **Kate Finnegan** Letters: **Oren Kramek**

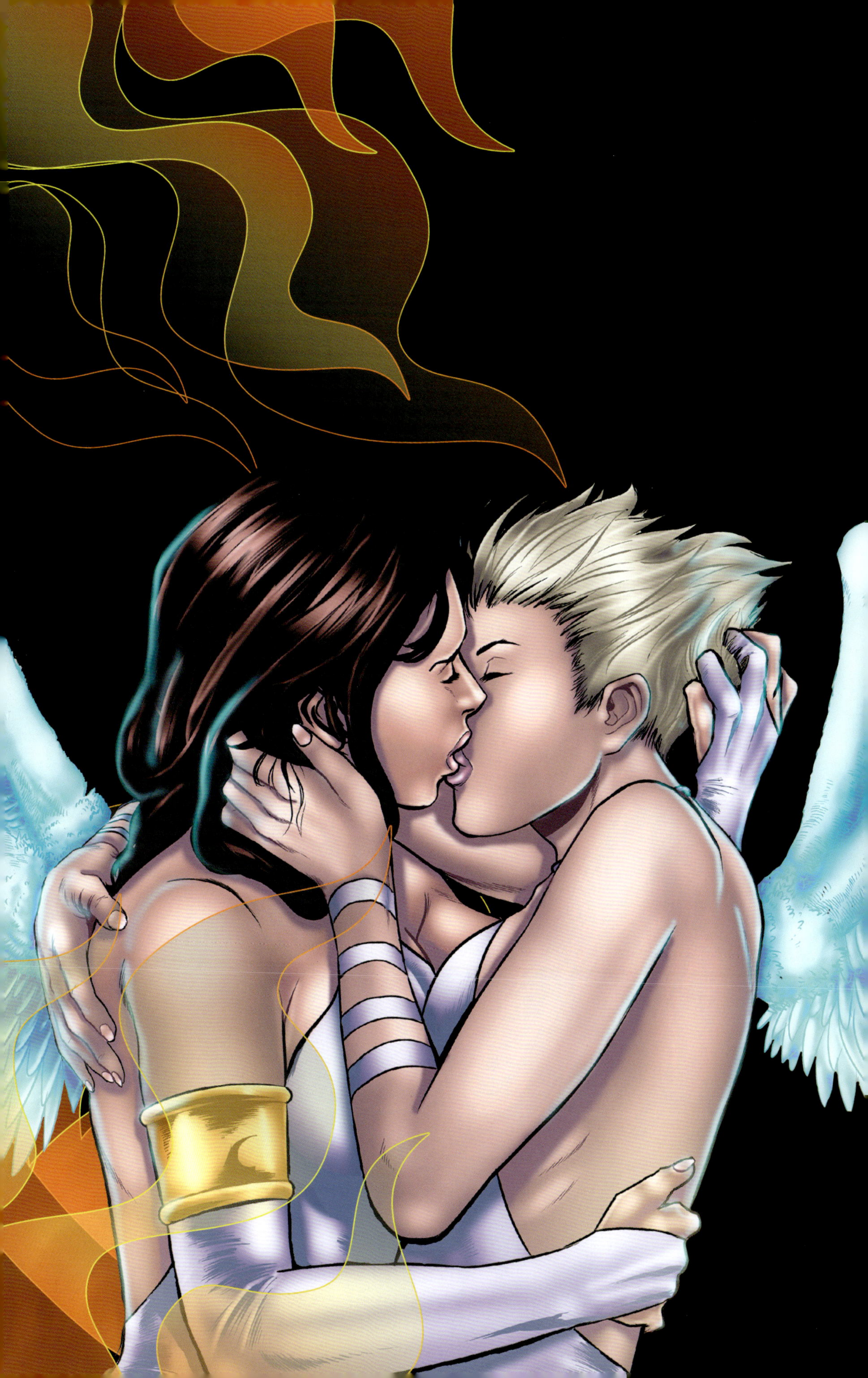

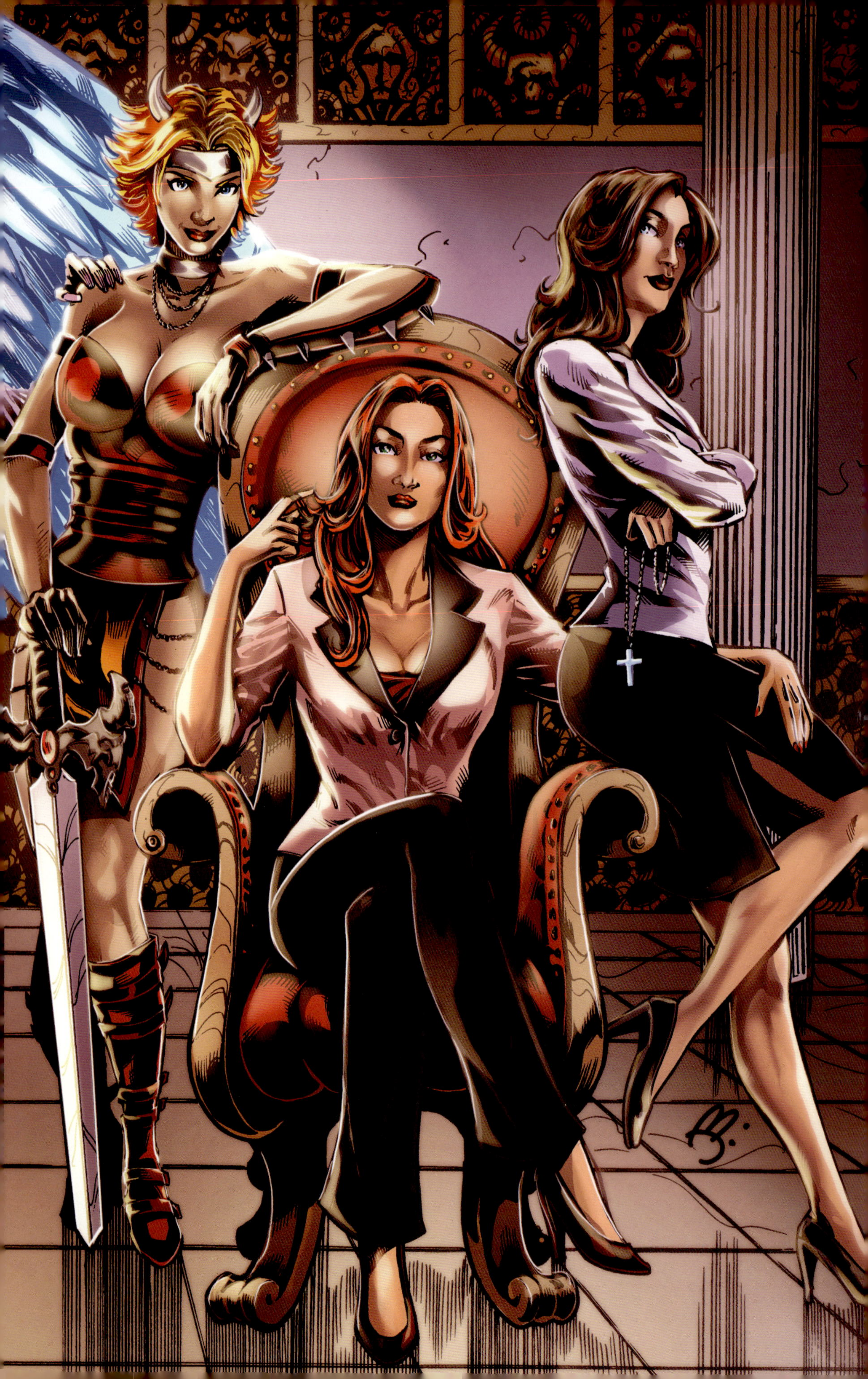

Mary Magdalene. What a beautiful name. Why did I ever decide to tease her by calling her Maggie? Lessons learned I suppose.

How she had the strength to do what she did...well...it's something I will never forget.

I should have been looking at the cross around her neck instead of her cleavage as we held that perverted demon down on the ground. Grinding his hips on my ass was bad enough, but that forked tongue of his was really creepy.

This journal wasn't my idea, but in the end I think it helped keep me sane even when sanity seemed to be a luxury.

Lessons learned...

DANICA!

"DANICA!"

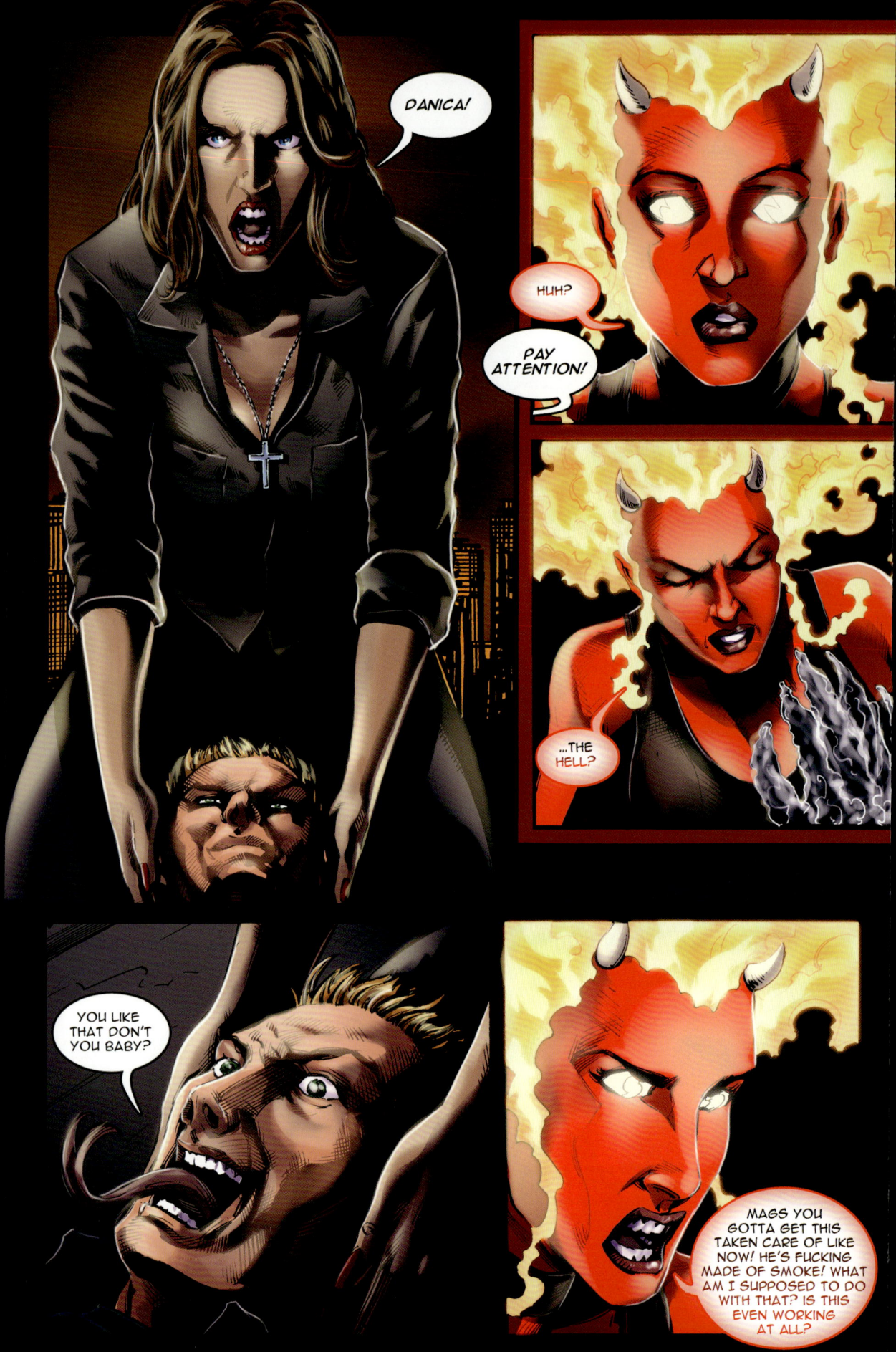

"HUH?"

"PAY ATTENTION!"

"...THE HELL?"

"YOU LIKE THAT DON'T YOU BABY?"

"MAGS YOU GOTTA GET THIS TAKEN CARE OF LIKE NOW! HE'S FUCKING MADE OF SMOKE! WHAT AM I SUPPOSED TO DO WITH THAT? IS THIS EVEN WORKING AT ALL?"

YES, I JUST NEED ANOTHER MINUTE.

I HOPE YOU'RE RIGHT...

Cause I don't think Bunny has a minute to spare!

YOU ARE STRONG! AND BEAUTIFUL AS WELL. YOU WILL BE A FINE ADDITION TO MY CONCUBINE STABLE.

MMMMM!

None of this happened as it should have.

As much as I prepared for it, I was nowhere near ready for the sheer power of Lucifer or the effect that War had on us all.

KNOCK KNOCK

"YES?"

"SORRY TO BOTHER YOU, MA'AM. I HAVE THE EMPLOYEE YOU REQUESTED HERE TO SEE YOU."

"GOOD. SEND HER IN."

"GOOD LUCK."

"THANKS A LOT."

"OK SO AM I FIRED OR WHAT?"

"FIRED? I OWN YOU. I CAN AND WILL USE YOU AS I SEE FIT. YOU'RE THE SPACE CADET THAT GOT RUN OVER BY A LAMBORGHINI IN THE VALET PARKING DRIVEWAY, RIGHT?"

"WELL... YES."

"AND I HEAR YOU'VE BEEN COMPLAINING ABOUT THE WARDROBE AT THE ETERNITY?"

"WELL, YEAH. I MEAN WE GET TO WEAR WHATEVER WE FIND IN THE WARDROBE DEPARTMENT BUT IT'S ALL HOOCHIE GEAR!"

"EVERYTHING IS DESIGNED TO MAKE US LOOK LIKE HOOKERS AND SLUTS. I KNOW THAT'S KIND OF THE VIBE YOU WANT TO PROJECT BUT A LITTLE BIT OF COMFORT GOES A LONG WAY WHEN YOU HAVE TO BE ON YOUR TOES ALL DAY LONG."

"YOU DO KNOW THERE'S MORE TO UNDERWEAR THAN THONGS AND PUSH UP BRAS, RIGHT?"

"AND WHAT ABOUT THOSE WINGS? I CHOSE THE DEVIL CHICK DEAL 'CAUSE THERE'S NO WAY IN HELL I'M CARRYING AROUND 30 POUNDS OF FEATHERS ALL DAY LONG! DO YOU KNOW HOW HEAVY THA—"

"WOULD YOU SHUT UP."

WHAT?
YOU HEARD ME. YOU WOULDN'T EVEN BE HERE RIGHT NOW IF NOT FOR YOUR DIVA PERSONALITY AND FASHION FETISH. YOU'RE BARELY WORTH MY TIME RIGHT NOW SO PAY ATTENTION AND DON'T MAKE ME REGRET GIVING A WHINEY LITTLE BITCH LIKE YOU THIS OPPORTUNITY.
TAKE THIS.
READ IT.
CAREFULLY.
YOU SCREW THIS UP AND I'LL MELT YOUR LIPS TOGETHER. THEN YOU WON'T HAVE TO WORRY ABOUT LOOKING LIKE A HOOKER ANYMORE WILL YOU?
NOW GET THE HELL OUT OF HERE.
JENNIE, MAKE SURE SOMEONE IS ON TOP OF THE CLEAN UP. WE HAVE TO BE DONE BEFORE SUNDOWN TONIGHT.
YES MA'AM.
AND I DON'T WANT TO BE DISTURBED TILL THE UTAH TEAM IS BACK.
YES MA'AM.

UTAH.

BUNNY.

BUNNY! ARE YOU OK?

THE POWER OF CHRIST...

HEY!

SORRY GIRLS. PLAYTIME IS OVER

YOU FORGET IT WAS THE POWER OF CHRIST THAT BROUGHT ME HERE.
USELESS WOMAN.
HOLD STILL SWEETHEART, OR THIS IS JUST GONNA END BAD FOR YOU.
BAD IS SO RELATIVE A TERM DON'T YOU THINK?
A LITTLE BAD NEVER HURT ANY-
URK!
WHAT'S THIS?
NOOOOO!
THE POWER OF CHRIST COMPELLS YOU!

YOU HARLOT! YOU'LL PAY DEARLY FOR THIS.

RETURN THAT SPIRIT TO ITS HOST...

NOW!

NO!

ARRRRGH!

DANICA NO!

DANICA ARE YOU OK?

NOoOOoo...

YOU FAIL TO GRASP THE REALITY OF THIS SITUATION MARY MAGDALENE. IT'S THE SWORD THAT MATTERS MOST OF ALL.

OH TRUST ME I'LL GIVE IT TO YA.

IF YOU MOVE AN INCH I'LL SNAP YOUR NECK AND TAKE THE SWORD MYSELF.

BUNNY DON'T LET GO OF THAT SWORD NO MATTER WHAT HAPPENS.

let it go

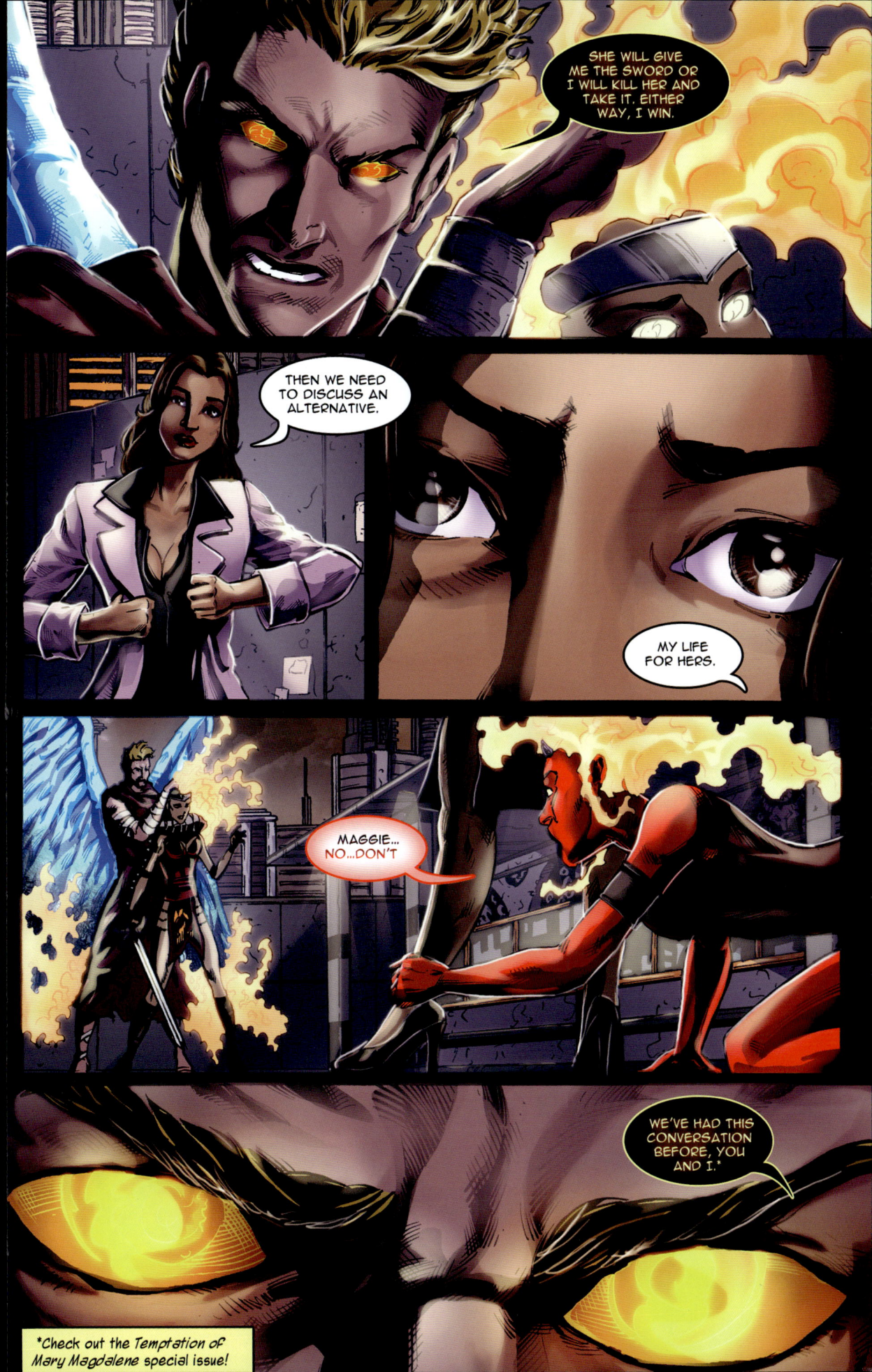

SHE WILL GIVE ME THE SWORD OR I WILL KILL HER AND TAKE IT. EITHER WAY, I WIN.

THEN WE NEED TO DISCUSS AN ALTERNATIVE.

MY LIFE FOR HERS.

MAGGIE... NO...DON'T

WE'VE HAD THIS CONVERSATION BEFORE, YOU AND I.*

*Check out the *Temptation of Mary Magdalene* special issue!

"WHAT I OFFERED YOU THEN WAS FAR GREATER THAN THE VALUE OF THIS LITTLE PEST."

"VALUE IS RELATIVE, LUCIFER. RELEASE HER AND THE SWORD AND I WILL COME WITH YOU."

"OR THE BELOVED OF YOUR MORTAL ENEMY?"

"WHAT'S WORTH MORE TO YOU? ANOTHER WEAPON OF WAR, ANOTHER "PEST" IN YOUR STABLE"

"AGREED."

MARY...

NO...

IT'S THE ONLY WAY. WE CAN'T BEAT HIM NOW. FINISH THE GAME AND DON'T FORGET ABOUT ME.

I'M HEADING TO THE BAR, JENNIE. MAKE SURE YOU GET YOURSELF TO THE GUF BY EIGHT O'CLOCK.
YES MA'AM.
TELL THE UTAH TEAM WHERE THEY CAN FIND ME WHEN THEY'RE DONE.
YES MA'AM.
I NEED A DRINK.
THUNK
30
12
L

I'VE GOT A COUPLE HOURS TO KILL. TIME TO DIG UP A LITTLE ENTERTAINMENT.

COURTNEY, YOU DON'T NEED TO BE DOING THAT.

IT'S MY JOB, MA'AM.

I KNOW, AND I APPRECIATE YOUR EFFORT. JUST GET TO THE GUF AND DON'T BE LEFT BEHIND.

THIS ISN'T WHAT WAS SUPPOSED TO HAPPEN...

NO ONE WAS SUPPOSED TO GO BACK HERE.

IT'S OK. I'LL BE FINE.

IT'LL GIVE ME SOME TIME TO PRACTICE WITH THIS SWORD SO WHEN YOU COME BACK FOR ME I CAN REALLY HELP YOU.

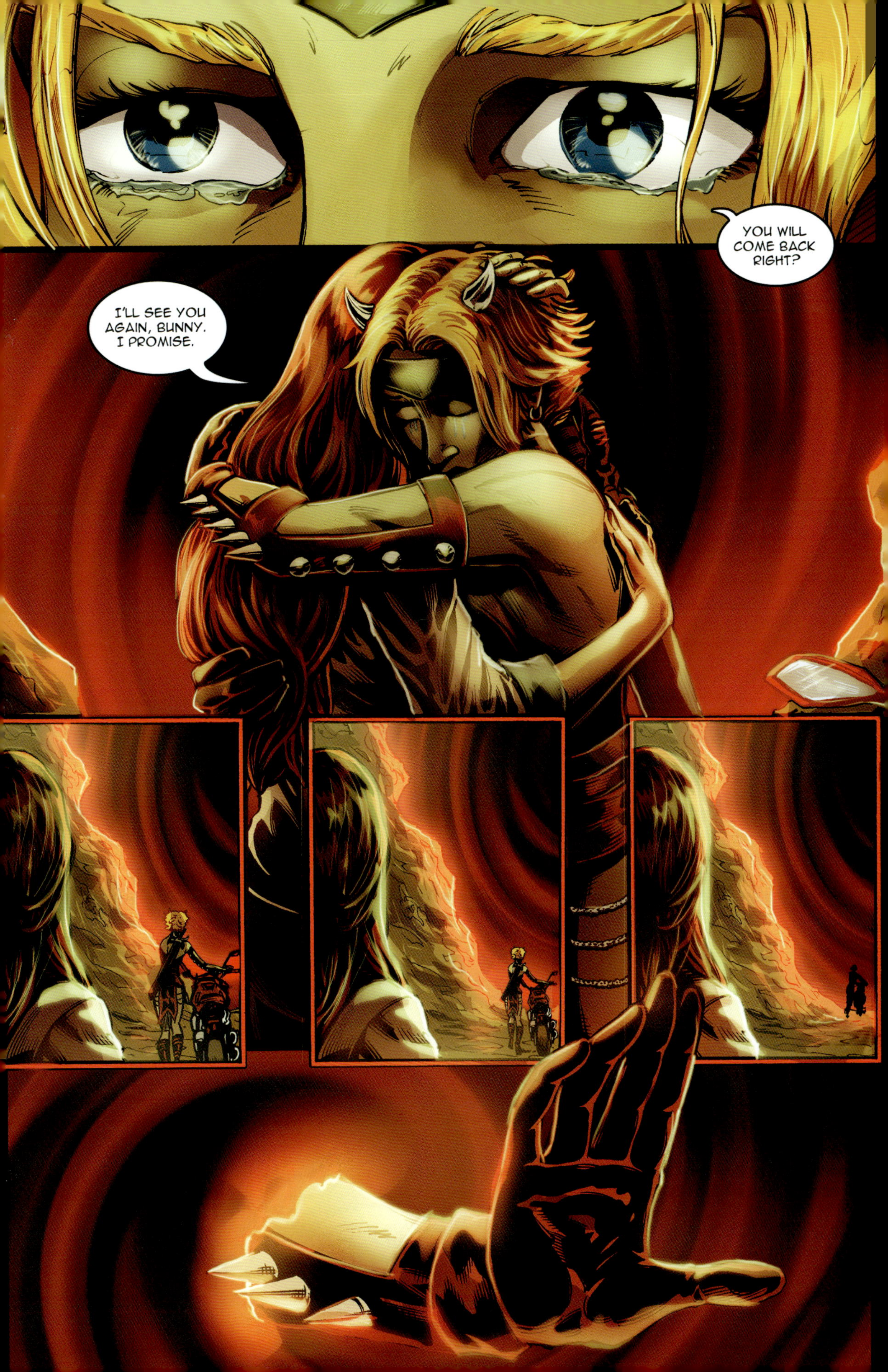
YOU WILL COME BACK RIGHT?
I'LL SEE YOU AGAIN, BUNNY. I PROMISE.

DANICA?
HEY! DANICA! WAKE UP!
WHAT THE HELL DO YOU WANT, SAM?
I WANT OUT! YOU'RE NOT EVEN WATCHING SO WHAT'S THE POINT?
YOU JUST DON'T GET IT DO YOU? YOU'RE HERE BECAUSE YOU CHOSE TO BE. YOU SOLD YOURSELF TO ME AND YOU'RE GONNA DO WHAT YOU'RE TOLD FOR THE REST OF TIME SO GET USED TO IT AND SHAKE THAT ASS RIGHT!
I DIDN'T AGREE TO BE TURNED INTO A DOUBLE D BIMBO, DANICA.
YOU WANT OUT SAM? REALLY?

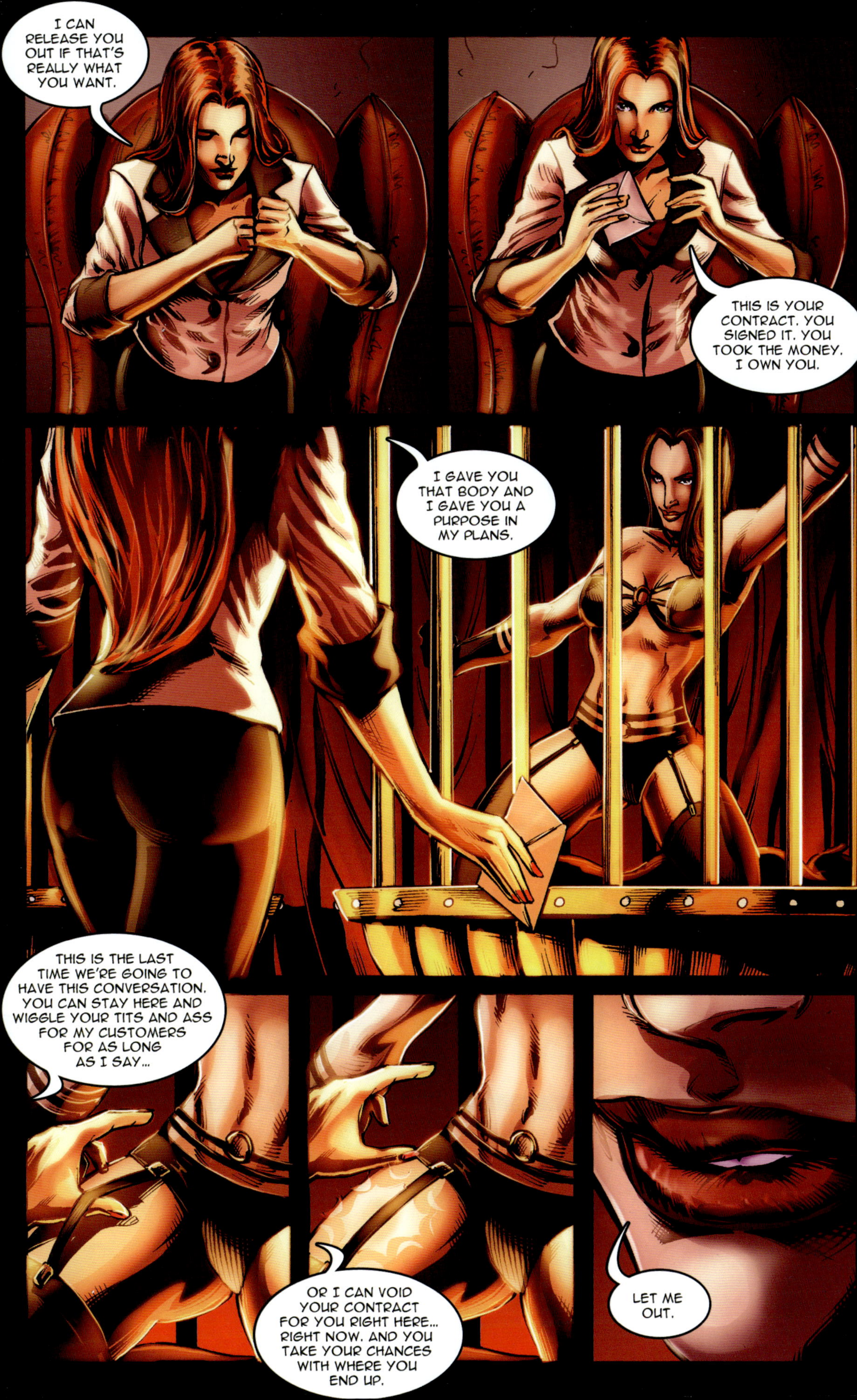
I CAN RELEASE YOU OUT IF THAT'S REALLY WHAT YOU WANT.
THIS IS YOUR CONTRACT. YOU SIGNED IT. YOU TOOK THE MONEY. I OWN YOU.
I GAVE YOU THAT BODY AND I GAVE YOU A PURPOSE IN MY PLANS.
THIS IS THE LAST TIME WE'RE GOING TO HAVE THIS CONVERSATION. YOU CAN STAY HERE AND WIGGLE YOUR TITS AND ASS FOR MY CUSTOMERS FOR AS LONG AS I SAY...
OR I CAN VOID YOUR CONTRACT FOR YOU RIGHT HERE... RIGHT NOW. AND YOU TAKE YOUR CHANCES WITH WHERE YOU END UP.
LET ME OUT.

NICE KNOWING YOU SAM.

WHAT THE...?

NOOO!

MA'AM, THE UTAH TEAM IS FINISHED.

GOOD. GET TO THE GUF AND LET EVERYONE YOU SEE ON THE WAY KNOW IT'S TIME TO WRAP THIS UP.

YES MA'AM.

"I'll get things ready for the Eternity's final visitors."

"NO I INSIST. AFTER YOU."

"FINE. LET'S JUST GET THIS OVER WITH."

"WELCOME TO THE ETERNITY, GENTLEMEN."

"A PLEASURE, DANICA."

"YES, ASSUMING OUR BUSINESS CONCLUDES TODAY AND IS NOT DRAGGED OUT FURTHER."

"UNLESS THERE IS ALTERNATIVE BUSINESS YOU'RE INTERESTED IN DISCUSSING OF COURSE..."

"OH PLEASE. YOU'RE DISGUSTING."

"I'LL TAKE YOU DOWNSTAIRS TO THE GUF. WE CAN DIVVY UP THE SOULS BETWEEN THE TWO OF YOU WHEN WE GET THERE."

"IS THERE A DRAFT ORDER WE SHOULD CONSIDER?"

"CAN YOU TAKE THIS SERIOUSLY FOR EVEN A MINUTE, LUCIFER?"

IF YOU DON'T WANT THE FIRST PICK I WILL HAPPILY ACCEPT IT.
WE'LL FLIP A COIN ALRIGHT? SATISFIED?
QUITE.
THE INQUISITION, HERE WE GO! THE INQUISITION, WHAT A SHOW! .
IS THAT REALLY NECESSARY?
JUST TRYING TO LIGHTEN THE MOOD MY FRIEND.
-DING-
GROOVY MOOD LIGHTING, DANICA

"YOU FLASHING BACK TO YOUR HIPPIE DAYS?"

"I HAVE SEEN THIS BEFORE."

"NO IT'S FAR MORE THAN THAT."

"YOU'VE DECEIVED US!"

"NO SHIT."

"OOF!"

"WHAT...?"

Sin City. My kind of town.

But you've heard this before. So I'll just remind you of one simple thing.

The only one who ever truly wins in this town...

IS ME!

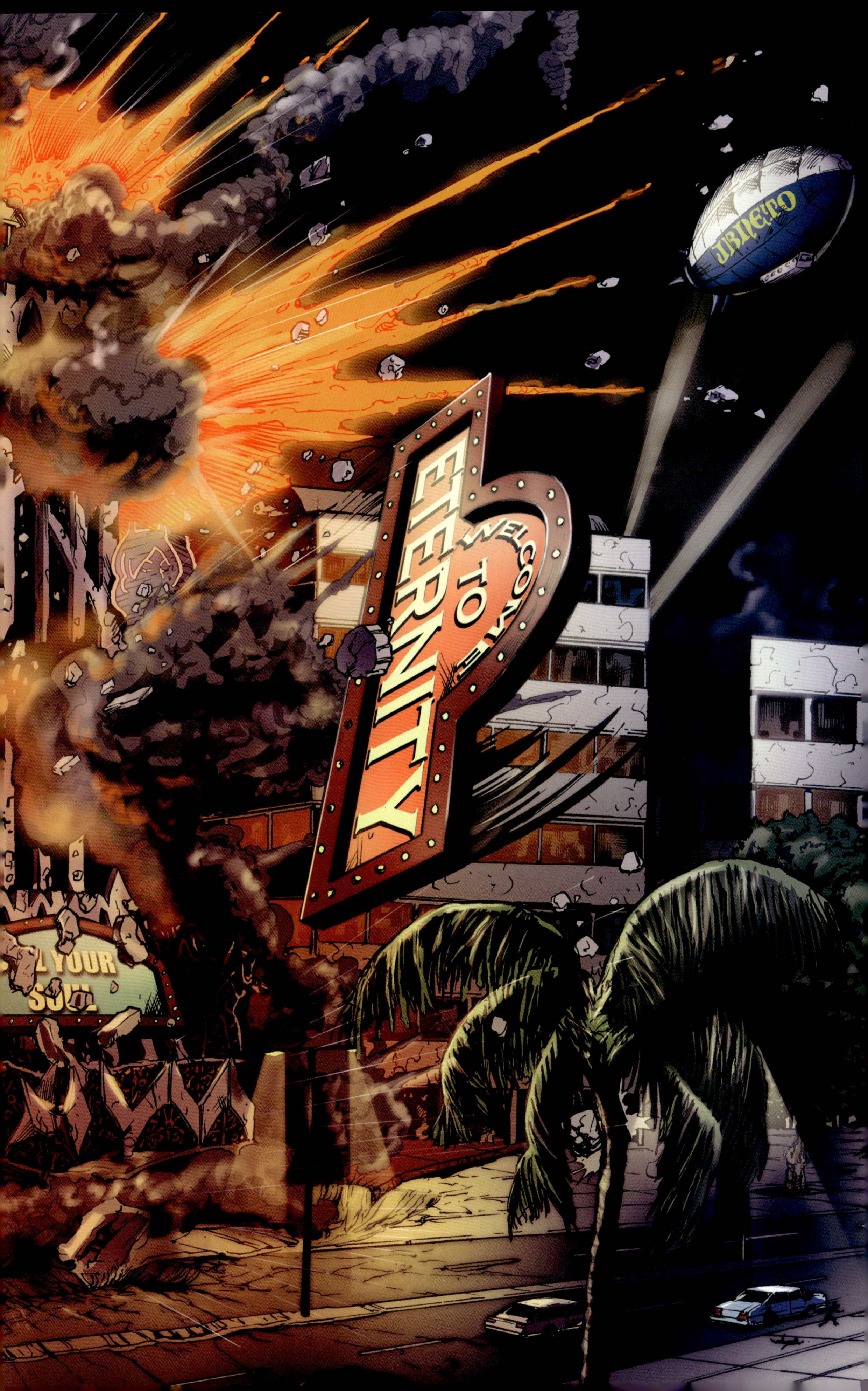
WELCOME TO ETERNITY
YOUR
SOUL

Epilogue...

COUGH COUGH!

GOOD GOD. WHAT DID SHE DO TO ME?

WE HAVE RECEIVED WORD THAT THE ETERNITY WAS DESTROYED, LORD DAMIEN.

FATHER MUST HAVE HAD ENOUGH OF THAT WRETCHED WOMAN'S INTERFERING AND TAKEN MATTERS INTO HIS OWN HANDS.

VOICES. MAYBE THEY CAN HELP GET ME OUT OF HERE.

LITTLE HELP HERE PLEASE...

HELLO?

NO MY LORD YOU MISUNDERSTAND. LORD LUCIFER WAS INSIDE WHEN THE BUILDING EXPLODED AND COLLAPSED TO THE GROUND.

AN INTERESTING TURN OF EVENTS WOULDN'T YOU SAY, VASSAGO?

AND JESUS?

THE LAMB WAS PRESENT AS WELL, LORD.

WHAT THE...

HA HA HA!

SHOW US YOUR SKILLS WOMAN.

A TASTY MORSEL INDEED.

THUNK

OW!

HEY THIS POLE IS COVERED IN THORNS. I CAN'T DO ANYTHING WITH THIS.

STUPID FEMALE. WHERE DID YOU THINK YOU WERE? THIS IS HELL, AND I JUST INHERITED THE THRONE!

YOU WILL PROVIDE THE EVENING'S ENTERTAINMENT EITHER ON A POLE OF THORNS, OR A BED OF THORNS.

CHOOSE.

YES SIR.

Writer: **Tom Hutchison** Artist: **Ian Snyder** Colors: **Kate Finnegan** Letters: **Oren Kramek**

The Devil's in the Details

Designing the Devil's granddaughter was not something I had envisioned doing at any point in my lifetime, but once in my head she would not let me go. When it came time to design Danica, I knew she would have to have a few different looks. After all she was not just a shapeshifting demon, but also had to play the part of a Las Vegas casino owner who sometimes took to the stage herself to convince the more difficult souls to sign on the dotted line. Artist John Rauch and I went over the basic ideas I had in mind and I let him flesh our heroine out. As it happens, the business skirt suit was used as Maggie's design and Danica instead wears the pants in our story. The overall suit style was used as the Eternity Hotel's official dress code with simple changes like different colored shirts under the jackets. Series artist J.B. Neto came in and designed the look of the hotel itself then took what John and I designed character wise and really made it his own. Over the course of 7 issues, J.B. took Danica, Maggie and the rest of the Eternity staff to creative heights I could not have imagined. Every page shows his growth throughout this series, and I for one am very much looking forward to his work on The False Prophet.

Without J.B. Neto, Penny for Your Soul may not even exist, and if it did it would certainly not be as good as it is today. J.B. took this job two years ago and to be honest, despite the tryout pages he did, I really didn't know what to expect. What I got was a man who put everything he had into my project. J.B. fills every page with such amazing detail and drama that you have to go back over each issue multiple times just to really be able to appreciate everything he has done. He took a chance on me as much as I did on him and for that I am truly greatfull. As we continue to work together, I have come to the belief that there is no one on this planet that would have been a better fit for this book than J.B. Every day that I receive new pages in my email is like Christmas. Watching him evolve his style and grow artistically from issue to issue has been a real treat. Unfortunately we have had some pieces J.B. has drawn that we just didn't have space for. I am very happy to be able to share a few of them here.

J.B. Neto Is The Heart of Penny For Your Soul.